BROKEN

CIN MEDLEY

MED'S PUB
PUBLISHING

BROKEN

Cin Medley

For Teresa
Thank you for the inspiration!

In what we perceive to be our darkest hour of life, what seems to be the end for our very soul is in fact a time to hope.

Is it possible to hope when death is upon you? Is it possible to hope that life is stronger and that the impossible becomes possible?

We find it within ourselves to survive, no matter the cost, but what if the cost is the opposite of everything that you are? What if you are so broken that you forget what is right?

To survive the darkness of terror, the fear of living, we find it within our very souls to do what is necessary to take one more breath. Live one more hour. Pray one more prayer.

We find it within ourselves to not let death win.

Broken
CIN MEDLEY

Published by: Med's Pub Publishing
Copyright © 2015 Cin Medley
All rights reserved
ISBN-13-978-0-9861178-6-2
ISBN-10-0986117862
Cover by: Amanda Walker PA & Design Services
Editing by: Kendra's editing and book services-Kendra Gaither

CHAPTER ONE

TATE

"Listen, there was a huge accident out on fifty-five, and traffic was diverted. I'm going to be about an hour behind. Jesus Christ, I can't see a fucking thing out here," Tate said into his phone.

"Be careful, man. I hate fucking storms like this. Bad shit always happens when the weather turns this rough," Josh told his long-time friend.

Tate Miles runs a private security company, and Josh Holden is his best friend and second in command. They've known one another for ten years, having been in the Navy together for eight of those years, then going through SEAL training. After a major conflict with terrorists in a war-ravaged country, they opted out of the SEALs and have been doing private security since.

"Yeah, I know what you mean," Tate shot back. "But there isn't anything I can do about it right now. Get a hold of Kelly for me and let her know that I'm running late."

Kelly Miles is Tate's little sister.

"No problem, buddy," Josh assured him.

"What the fuck?" Tate watched as an oncoming car swerved from the other side of the road into his lane. "Shit, I gotta go!" He hung up, dropping his phone in his lap, and grabbed the steering wheel with both hands.

The car was heading his way fast, jerking along the road and sliding on the wet pavement. Tate slowed his own and jerked the wheel, sending his car sliding sideways down the road before turning it around so it was facing the opposite direction. "Fuck," he yelled as the car came to a stop.

Gathering his bearings, he looked out the windshield, where he could see the brake lights from the other car flicking on and off then on again. It looked like the car had come to a stop. Tate pushed on the gas pedal, moving toward the car to see if he could help, but stopped short when he saw what looked like a woman jump out of the passenger side and take off running. He opened his door just as the driver side door opened and a man jumped out, running after the girl. He tackled her to the pavement, and Tate moved to get out of his car. Standing in the pouring rain, he could hear the woman screaming as the man grabbed her by the hair and dragged her back to the car.

As he stood there in the downpour, Tate had a flashback to Kelly. He watched while her husband did the same thing, only they weren't in the road. They were in her living room, and Tate was standing outside on the porch.

It was surreal. Standing there watching the scene unfold right before his eyes, he couldn't distinguish between real and memory.

The woman being dragged in front of him managed to trip up the guy pulling her. "Fucking bitch!" he yelled as he hit the pavement.

Tate snapped out of his memory just as the man lifted his fist to swing at the woman. He hit her four maybe five times before Tate was moving toward them.

"Hey," he yelled at the guy. But he didn't stop. He just kept swinging, hitting her in the face, chest, and back. Tate took off running, and the moment he got within reach, grabbed the guy by the shirt and pulled him off her.

"What the fuck? Stay out of this, man," the guy shouted.

Tate spun around to face him. "What is your problem? You don't beat up on women like that." He could feel his anger brewing, barely able to keep it just below the surface.

"That bitch belongs to me so stay the fuck out of this!" The man shook himself loose from Tate's grip and moved toward the woman again.

Tate stepped in front of him. "No!"

The guy reached behind him and swung his arm around, holding a gun. "I said to walk away, motherfucker."

Tate grabbed the gun and punched the guy in the face. The gun went off as the man staggered back, the bullet slicing through the upper bicep of Tate's left arm, giving him a hell of a flesh wound. He kept hitting him and hitting him. With the memories flooding his mind of Kelly's husband, he couldn't stop himself until the moaning in his mind froze him in mid-swing. Dropping the gun, Tate turned around to see the woman dragging herself away. Looking back at the gun lying on the road, then back to the woman, Tate stood and walked over to her. The memory of Kelly's face took center stage in his mind.

"I am so sorry," he whispered as he bent down and picked her up. "I am so sorry for not being here." He pulled the woman to his chest and carried her to his car, gently slipping her in the front seat, before jumping in and taking off.

His phone rang, and he nearly crashed trying to find it.

"What the fuck, man? Is everything all right?" Josh sounded frantic.

"No, man, I need you to meet me at the cabin and bring the doc with you. Shit just got real." That was his and Josh's tell-tale phrase for one another when they were in trouble.

"Meet you there," Josh said and hung up.

Tate didn't stop driving until he got to the cabin. It was dark, and the storm was still raging. The cabin was dark, so Josh and the doc still hadn't made it there. He got out of the car and walked around to the passenger side. Pulling the woman out, he carried her to the door, his arm throbbing from the gunshot wound. He managed to get the door open and kicked it shut as he moved through the cabin to his bedroom. He laid her on the bed and pulled off her shoes, jeans, and then her shirt and quickly covered her with blankets.

He went to the bathroom, pulled off his clothes, and dried off. Grabbing some boxers and sweats, he went back to check out his arm. Shaking his head, he wrapped a towel around it and went to the kitchen.

Tate hadn't had a drink since the night he killed Kelly's husband, but tonight, he needed one. He reached for the cabinet above the stove and grabbed a bottle of Jack. After pouring a tumbler full, he downed it and then another. He filled the tumbler again and took the bottle and glass to the bedroom.

Sitting it down on the table next to the chair, he walked over to the bed. Reaching down, he gently moved her hair from her face. It was a bloody mess. Tate shook his head and went to sit in the chair to wait for Josh and the doc while the storm raged on outside.

His mind clouded over again, remembering the night he walked up to see his sister after drinking with his buddies. Tate had been home on leave from his last deployment and was out drinking with Josh and the guys when he decided it was time to crash, so he headed to Kelly's. As he walked up, he could hear her husband, John, screaming at her. Tate had been on the porch, looking in the window, when he saw Kelly come flying out of the kitchen and landing on her back not ten feet from where he stood. John came out and grabbed her by the hair, and as he started to drag her back into the kitchen, Kelly woke up and fought to get away from him. Tate froze as he watched John punch her a few times in the face.

His feet were moving, and he kicked in the front door before grabbing John by the neck and punching him in the face. John tried to fight back, but Tate had been drinking and was out of control. He literally beat John to death. After the last blow, he turned to see Kelly lying on the floor covered in blood. He carried her out to the car, put her in the passenger seat, and drove her to the hospital. She was in surgery for nine hours to repair the damage that fucker did to her. As she recovered, Tate sat in the dark, watching her sleep, listening to the machines working to keep her alive. The police had showed up a few times to question him. They wanted Kelly's side, but the detective had assured him that it was self-defense.

Tate's phone dinged, and he snapped his head around. He got up and went to the bathroom, fishing it out of his jeans. Turning it on, he saw a text from Josh.

Almost there, buddy.

Tate went back into the bedroom, picking up his glass as he walked through to the living room. He stood in front of the huge window and waited. Headlights lit the room and moved across the walls as Josh pulled in, and another car pulled in right behind him. Tate smiled; Josh brought the guys with him. He walked over and opened the door, stepping out onto the porch, watching as four men got out of each vehicle.

Josh was first on the porch. "What the hell happened?"

Then everyone followed. Tate just turned and walked into the cabin. He set his glass on the kitchen island as everyone crowded around. Josh looked at his glass and then at him. He knew it was bad because Tate hadn't had a drink in ten years.

"Doc, I need you to come with me. The rest of you, set up and stay put. We'll be back in a few."

Tate turned and walked away, the doc following him. Josh and the rest of guys went about setting up their computers, while Tate pushed open the bedroom door.

"Doc, you need to check her out. Make sure she's going to survive." Tate's voice sounded anxious even to himself.

Doc looked at him, and then Tate left to go back out to talk to Josh. He filled them all in on what had happened.

"I need you to get some guys out there and find this bastard. I wrote down his plate number, so find out who he is and get him in. Something isn't right here."

"Tate man?" Josh nodded to his glass.

Tate smiled. "Yeah, buddy, this shit just got real. I'm all right, just need to calm my nerves. The memories are a bitch."

Josh nodded. "I know, man, just be careful with that shit."

Tate brought the glass to his mouth and threw back the rest of the Jack in it. "Yeah, I'm done now." He set the glass on the counter and headed back to the bedroom.

He sat in the chair and watched Doc check her over. "Here, Tate, help me roll her over. Something's not right here. She has a huge cut across her hip, and I can't see around her back."

Tate got up and kneeled on the bed. He put one hand on her hip and the other on her shoulder and pulled her toward him. She was so light and thin; her ribs were very visible. Tate closed his eyes and swallowed hard.

"Oh fuck," Doc said.

"What?" Tate leaned over and nearly lost the contents of his stomach. The woman had slices cut through her back. "Those are whip marks. Someone whipped her." He held her while Doc cleaned her up. Then he gently laid her down and moved her hair off her face. He couldn't help but notice the bruises on her chest and legs. He got off the bed and walked calmly out of the room, through the cabin, and out into the raging storm. His fist found the beam that held up the porch, the bones in his hand cracking under the pressure. He walked out into the storm and looked up at the dark sky. "Fuck!"

Josh had followed him out and was standing on the porch watching him. Tate didn't move; he just stood there. Josh went back in when Doc came out of the bedroom.

"What the fuck is going on?" he asked Doc.

"There is a young woman in the bedroom," Doc replied.

"What? Who is she?"

Doc shook his head. "I have no idea, but she's been tortured." He lowered his voice so only Josh could hear him. "She has some pretty bad looking lash marks from being whipped."

Josh spun around to look at Tate in the yard. "No fucking way," he whispered.

The silence was long. No one moved. Even the sounds of their breaths couldn't be heard over their thoughts. Tate turned around and saw Josh looking at him. *They know,* he thought to himself. Tate closed his eyes and swallowed. Shaking his head, he started back to the cabin. He didn't stop to chat, just went right back to the bedroom and pushed the door closed behind him. He went to the bathroom and dried himself off again and put on another pair of sweats then got comfortable in the chair.

The guys went searching for the guy who shot Tate. He was gone when they arrived at the scene. When they located the car, a few of them took off to hunt the guy down.

Josh didn't tell anyone what he knew. Tate was his friend and his boss, and there was no way he could betray him, not after everything Tate had done for him. Josh picked up an ink pad and some paper and went to knock on the bedroom door. Pushing the door open, he said, "Hey, man, I'm going to take her fingerprints. Maybe she's in the system somewhere. She might be a missing person or something."

Tate nodded. He knew it was the right thing to do, but he didn't want anyone to touch her. "I'll do it." He got up and took the ink pad. Carefully, he picked up her hand. Her fingernails were broken off and jagged. The tips of the fingers on her right hand were bloody. Reaching over, he picked up her left hand, pressed her thumb into the ink, and rolled her fingerprint onto the pad of paper. He handed it back to Josh. "As soon as you know, let me know."

Josh nodded and left. Tate went back to the bed. He looked down at her frail beaten body and whispered, "Don't worry, you are safe now." He made his way back to the chair and sat down.

It was difficult to shut off his brain. Memories have the ability to keep you happy when you're sad, or they can scare the hell out of you on dark stormy nights like this one. For Tate, it was easy to shut them off and put them away. But when reality showed its ugly face, it was difficult at best to keep them where they couldn't hurt him.

The Jack Daniels finally kicked in, and Tate closed his eyes slowly. Sleep finally won. Doc had come in and set up an I.V. for the woman, giving her fluids and antibiotics. He was quiet, making sure not to wake Tate. Josh had come in a few times, but Tate kept sleeping. The storm had moved on and the sun was breaking in the sky. The guys had found the man that shot Tate and beat the woman and were holding him in a warehouse downtown. Josh had discovered who the woman was and needed to wake Tate.

Tate's eyes opened slowly as the sun crossed his face. He looked at the tiny woman in the bed and realized that he was not dreaming. Pushing himself out of the chair, he walked over to the bed. He saw the I.V. in her arm and trailed the line up to the bag. He moved her hair off her face and whispered, "Who are you, beautiful?"

Josh cleared his throat. "I know who she is," he said softly.

Tate turned and walked out of the room. "Talk to me," he said.

"Well, we have the guy who shot you in a warehouse downtown."

"Bring him out here. Take him to the shed." Tate looked at his friend. "What else?"

"The car is registered to a guy named Blake Sully. He owns a few strip clubs downtown."

Tate crinkled his eyebrows. "I've heard of this guy. He's a real bastard to the women who work for him. Claims he owns them." He turned to look at the bedroom door.

Josh shook his head. "No, man, she doesn't work for him. Her name is Teresa Barns. She's been missing for six months. Get this, she is an Assistant District Attorney."

Tate looked at him. "What the fuck was she doing with Sully? Find her family and get them out."

"We're working on that now. Hey, man, Kelly called a few times. She isn't happy about you missing Taylor's party."

Tate smiled. Taylor was his four-year-old niece. He would literally move the moon for her. Turning four was a big deal for her. Tate pulled his phone out of his back pocket. Dialing Kelly's number, he walked out onto the porch.

"Oh, someone better have died, or I am not talking to you," she yelled into the phone.

Tate smiled then got serious. "I need you, Kel. I'm out at the cabin. Can you come?"

She got real quiet. "I'll take Tay to the sitters and come right away. Tate, are you all right?"

"Yes and no. Please, be careful," he whispered and hung up.

Kelly knew the same secrets as Tate. She wore a few of the same scars, too.

CHAPTER TWO

TERESA BANS

"I won't forget. I promise," Teresa said, smiling and shaking her head.

"I love you, baby. The things I am going to do to you this weekend... I just love those lacy black panties of yours," Ted told her.

"I love you, too." She got in the elevator as she ended the call.

Teresa was new to the world of ADA's, but she was good at her job. Her six-month investigation into the rumors about Blake Sully was coming to an end. Turns out, he was more involved with the human trafficking of young girls into sex rings than any of them could have imagined. She had compiled enough evidence to have him indicted.

Putting herself in great danger, she had infiltrated one of his many clubs around the city. Her boyfriend and lead detective into the investigation, Ted Hardt, made sure she was as safe as she could be without breaking her cover.

Now, she had all the evidence she needed to take her findings to the Grand Jury to indict him and send him away for a very long time. Everything was ready for the raid, which would save probably hundreds of young women who had been kidnapped and traded into the sex trade.

The elevator pinged, and Teresa stepped off into the hallway. As she came around the corner and headed toward the courtroom to the hearing, a man in a suit walked up to her in a panic.

"Excuse me, can you please help me? My daughter ran into the bathroom, and I can't seem to get her out. She was very upset. Her boyfriend was just sentenced to five years, and she threatened to kill herself," he said.

"Of course, where is she?" Teresa's heart went out to this man who was visibly upset.

"Down the hall, there." He pointed to the ladies' room down the hall in the opposite direction of the courtroom.

Teresa looked at her watch, making sure she had plenty of time to help. She followed the man down the hall.

Teresa smiled at the man and pushed through the door he'd indicated. It was eerily quiet in the restroom. "Hello," she said. All the doors to the stalls were open. She turned to go back out, but the man was standing behind her.

His hand came up and covered her mouth. "Your boyfriend and his entire precinct are going to die if you do not come with me right now. I have the whole place wired to blow if you fight me. Do you understand?"

She nodded. He let go of her face and pulled her out of the restroom, but not before she dropped her purse on the floor. They took the stairs down to the parking garage where a black SUV was waiting for them. He shoved her inside, and another man put a black bag over her head before they sped away.

"What do you want?" she asked.

"Someone wants to see you," one of the men said with a menacing chuckle.

Teresa was scared, but this was something Ted would do. Although, she had to be in court, and he wouldn't do this knowing what was on the docket today. They had worked hard to get this evidence; he wouldn't jeopardize this investigation. The SUV slowed down and then came to a stop. When the doors opened, Teresa could smell oil. Where the hell was she?

One of the guys grabbed her and roughly pulled her out of the car.

She fell to the ground, and he grabbed her under the arm and jerked her to her feet, pushing her forward. They walked a short distance, and then he made her stop.

"What the fuck?" she said, just as a hand slapped her across the face, sending a blinding pain through her head. She felt a hand grab the black bag and pull it off, ripping some of her hair out in the process.

Teresa tried to adjust her eyes, but before she could, another slap seared across her face.

"What the fuck is your problem?" she screamed out.

She heard someone chuckle, and not a happy chuckle but a scary demonic chuckle. "You've been a busy little girl, haven't you Miss Barns, special Investigative Assistant District Attorney."

She flipped her head up, ready to do battle, but he punched her in the stomach and she doubled over in pain. He knocked the wind right out of her. "You think you can walk into my world and change it? You apparently have no idea who the fuck I am."

"What are you talking about?" She gasped for air through the pain.

He threw her files on the ground in front of her. Then he squatted down, grabbing her by the hair. "You fucking know what I'm talking about. Now, I'll have the pleasure of showing you, teaching you all about it." He pushed her head down to the floor. "Take this bitch back to the office. Time to break in an ADA. This should be fun." The man walked away, and Teresa watched his feet climb in the car. *There is no way Blake Sully just kidnapped me.*

A guy grabbed her by the arm and pulled the black bag over her head again. "Come on, guys, do you know who I am? The cops are going to be looking for me. Just let me go and I will forget I know you." She tried not to sound scared shitless as she attempted to reason with them. She didn't see it coming, but one of the guys swung, hitting her square in the jaw and knocking her out.

"Shut the fuck up," he said as she collapsed onto the concrete floor.

Picking her up, he threw her over his shoulder, and the other guy opened the back of the SUV so he could throw her in. They drove back to the club and hauled her downstairs into Sully's favorite place. It's where he broke in all his girls.

Sully never sold a girl without trying her out first. He said it was his policy, so he didn't sell defective goods, so he would work them over in his favorite room. When they walked in, Sully was sitting in his leather chair across the room, smoking a cigar and drinking his whiskey.

"Strip her and put her on the racks," he told his goons, as he sat there getting hard, watching them tear her clothes from her body. "Leave those panties on her."

One guy held her up while the other wrapped the restraints around her wrists. Then she was lifted and hung on a rack suspended from the ceiling, her feet just touching the floor.

"Now, get the fuck out of here," Sully shouted.

They left, closing the door behind them. He put his cigar down and stood, removing his jacket and shirt, hanging them on the back of the chair. Bending down, he picked up the bucket of ice water off the floor and walked over to Teresa, throwing it on her.

Her body jumped, and she twisted around in her restraints. Sully chuckled that demonic chuckle. Teresa looked up at him as he said, "Welcome back, Sandy. I went far too easy on you while you worked here. You know," he walked closer and pinched her nipple, "I knew I should have invited you down here before I let you take the stage. If I had, none of this would be happening." He twisted the other nipple, causing her to scream out from pain. He chuckled. "You like that, baby?"

A second later, he slammed a wooden paddle along the backs of her thighs, and a searing pain shot through her body. Teresa screamed. "That's it, let it all go," he whispered in her ear. Teresa slammed her head into his face, breaking his nose. "Fuck!"

Teresa smiled, knowing she'd caused him pain. She knew he was going to kill her, but she was determined to take a piece of him with her. "Fuck you, bastard!" she screamed at him.

He grabbed her by the hair, pulling her face right up in front of his. "Oh, I am going to fuck every orifice on this beautiful fucking body of yours, and then I am going to have the pleasure of slitting your fucking throat."

Teresa spit in his face, and Sully slammed his fist into her face, knocking her out.

Walking over to the sink, he gripped his nose between his fingers and jerked it back into place. "Fuck!" he yelled. Turning on the water, he washed the blood from his hands and face. He filled the bucket again with water then walked over and threw it in Teresa's face. She jumped, choking on the water. He grabbed her face. "You ready for me?" he asked.

"Fuck you," she whispered.

He laughed. "If you insist."

CHAPTER THREE

Tate was sitting in the chair, staring at the shattered young woman in his bed, when the door opened.

"Hey, man, Kelly just pulled up," Josh said quietly.

"Thanks." Tate got up and walked into the living room and then out onto the porch. He watched as his sister's car pulled onto the lawn. She got out, and he met her in the yard, throwing his arms around her shoulders and nearly knocking her down.

"Tate, what is going on?" she whispered into his neck.

"The past never fucking stays where it should, Kel." he whispered back. Tate felt her stiffen in his embrace. "Come on, we need to talk." He released her, and they walked arm in arm to the cabin. Kelly said hi to the guys and then followed Tate into the bedroom. He closed the door quietly behind her.

"What is this?" she asked him.

Tate proceeded to tell her what happened, "She is an Investigative Assistant District Attorney. Her name is Teresa Barns, and she went missing six months ago."

"I remember hearing about her on the news. Her boyfriend is a detective, I think. Why haven't you taken her to the hospital? There has got to be people out there who are looking for her."

"I can't."

Kelly looked at him. "Tate, what aren't you telling me?"

He walked over to the bed and knelt next to her. Putting one hand on her shoulder and one on her hip, he gently rolled her onto her side. Kelly walked over very slowly to see what he was showing her.

"Uh, no," she whispered, backing away. She nearly fell over, reaching out for the wall to keep herself standing.

Tate gently laid Teresa down and rushed to his sister. Her whole body was shaking. When he wrapped his arms around her, she burst into tears, burying her face in his chest. "This can't be, Tate. This just can't be." She sobbed.

"I don't think it's the same. He's dead, Kel. I know because I killed him myself."

"Are you sure, Tate?"

"Pretty sure, yeah. After what he did to you and mom, I beat him pretty bad."

"Then who did this to her? Who has skills like that? In my whole life, I have never seen whip marks like ours, until now."

As she spoke the words, Tate could feel the burn across his back and thighs. Closing his eyes, the memories he had buried long ago seemed to come to the forefront of his mind. He was ten, and Kelly was just five. Tate had broken a plate on accident. He wasn't paying attention when he went to put it in the sink, and it fell to the floor.

His stepfather, Frank, shoved the table away from him, screaming, "You little son of a bitch! What do you think I'm made of? Fucking money?"

Tate cowered away from him, his mother intervening. "Frank, honey, it was an accident."

Tate jerked as he remembered the sound when Frank back-handed her, knocking her out of her chair. "I am so sick of you defending these brats. They need a good ass whipping!" Frank yelled, grabbing Tate by the neck. "Come on, you little fucker. You need to be taught a lesson."

Tate felt the tears well up in his eyes as he held his sister, the memory flooding his mind. Frank dragged him out of the house and through the yard to the garage. He opened the door and threw him inside. Tate landed face first on the cement. Standing there in his sister's arms, he could still recall the smell of old oil on the floor.

Frank grabbed his whip off the wall of the garage and swung it, striking Tate across the backs of his legs. "You little fucker, next time, you'll be more careful. Breaking my shit, you little bastard." He swung again, landing the whip on his thighs, slashing open his jeans along with the flesh under it. Tate had screamed in pain.

"Tate," Kelly said. "Tate." She shook him.

"Sorry, I was just remembering the first time."

"When you broke the plate," she whispered. "I remember hearing you screaming. I was so scared for you. I am so sorry he did those things to you." Kelly could never bring herself to say thank you to Tate for taking most of those whippings that were meant for her.

"It's in the past and we survived," he said sternly, not wanting her to know how he really felt. He is who he is now, and no one will ever hurt him again like that. "The guy who did this to her, we think his name is Blake Sully. The guys are doing their research into him."

"So, what did you need from me?"

"Kelly, when she wakes up, she's going to be freaking out. I'm sure that a big guy like me isn't what she'll want to see. I was hoping you could just stay here until she comes out of this and calms down enough to tell us what the hell happened to her. She needs protecting," Tate said.

"Leave it to my big brother to protect her." She smiled at him. "Of course, I'll stay."

Tate hugged her. "Thank you. I have some things to do. Doc is here. Text me when she wakes up."

"You've got it."

Tate stopped by the bed and gently moved Teresa's hair from her face, then walked out into the living room.

"Is he here yet?" he asked Josh.

"Yeah, the fucker is in the shed."

Tate grabbed a t-shirt off the couch and headed out the door. Josh and two other guys followed him out. As they were walking through the yard to the shed out back, Tate picked up a tree branch that had fallen during the storm. He broke all the little twigs off as he walked. Stopping at the door, he took a deep breath and opened it.

The guy was sitting in the middle of the room, tied and handcuffed to the chair, with a black cloth bag over his head. Tate grabbed another chair and put it on the floor directly in front of him.

"This is going to go one of two ways. First way, you tell me everything I want to know, and you won't go to prison an invalid. Second way, I will beat you within an inch of your life to get the information I want, and then I will decide if you live or die. Choose now."

"Fuck you," the guy yelled.

"Wrong answer," Tate said as he swung the piece of wood and connected with the guy's knee, sending him tumbling to the floor.

"Mother fucker!" the guy yelled.

Josh and Devlin picked him up and sat him back upright.

"I can see that you have chosen the second option. Who was the woman in your car?" Tate asked.

"Fuck you!"

Tate swung again, hitting the other knee, sending him to the floor again. Josh and Devlin picked him back up.

"Who was the woman in your car?"

The guy didn't answer, so Tate swung again, this time landing the thick branch across his forearm. The guy screamed out in pain.

"She's my property., I bought her fair and square." He yelled.

"Who did you buy her from? Better yet why did you buy her?" Tate was getting pissed.

"Some guy down town. I bought her for a client, she's been conditioned. Chicks like her love to be controlled." The guy was whimpering.

Tate had to control himself. He wanted to kill this guy, but he needed information. "Conditioned for what?"

The guy actually chuckled. "Like you don't know."

Tate slammed the branch across his other forearm, and everyone in the shed heard the guy's arm break.

17

"Oh! Fuck, man, you broke my arm. I told you what you wanted to know. What the fuck?"

Tate stood and punched the guy, knocking him out. "Are you fucking kidding me?" He looked at Josh. "This shit just got real. When he comes to, come and get me. I need a fucking drink." He dropped the branch and walked out of the shed.

On his way across the lawn, he noticed his hands were shaking. "Fuck," he whispered to himself. It was the scream that echoed through the trees that jerked his head toward the cabin. Everyone came running out of the shed, and Tate took off across the lawn, making it back to the cabin before the scream ended. He ran into the bedroom to find Teresa curled up in the corner of the room with Kelly trying to calm her down.

"Kelly, go wait in the kitchen."

Kelly left, and Tate sat on the floor. "My name is Tate Miles. I found you in the road. This is my cabin, and you are safe. I am not going to hurt you. That was my sister, Kelly."

She sat there crying and shaking in her bra and panties. Tate got up and grabbed the blanket off the bed, nodding to her and holding it out so she knew he was giving it to her. He moved closer, and she shook harder, so he dropped it on the floor in front of her and went back to where he was sitting.

"Teresa," he said to her. She looked at him with wild eyes. "I know who you are. Your name is Teresa Barns, and you are an ADA. You have been missing for six months." She cried harder. Tate moved a bit closer to her. "You have been beaten. The man who hurt you on the road is being taken care of." Her eyes shot up, full of even more panic. Tate moved a bit closer to her. "I am not going to hurt you. You pulled your I.V. out. I have a doctor here who has been taking care of your wounds, and the I.V. has medicine in it, antibiotics." She looked up at the pole and then to her arm where blood was seeping from the spot where the I.V. had been. "I promise you, no one is going to hurt you again." Tate made this promise from his heart. He knew he wouldn't let anything happen to her. He moved even closer to her. "Teresa?" She jerked her head up. "You have some serious gashes on your back.

Will you let the doc come in and put the I.V. back in so you can get your medicine? I would hate for you to get an infection after my brilliant rescue of you." He smiled at her. She nodded.

"Kelly, get Doc in here," he said without looking away. He knew she was still right outside the door.

A minute later, Doc came in. Tate did not take his eyes off her. "This is Doc. He's been taking care of you. He won't hurt you, I promise. He is going to clean up your arm and put your I.V. back in, all right?"

She nodded.

"Doc, move slow," he cautioned.

Doc came in and moved the pole over before sitting on the floor next to Teresa. Tate moved so he could maintain eye contact with her. Doc opened his case and went to touch her, but Teresa pulled her hand away and cowered in the corner.

"Teresa," Tate said softly. "Look at me, beautiful. He won't hurt you." She looked up at him. Doc reached for her arm, and this time, she didn't pull away. She let him clean her arm and then put in the new I.V. When he was done, he slowly moved away, giving Tate a strange look.

"See, now, would you like to get back in bed, or use the bathroom, or have something to eat?" She nodded. Tate smiled at her. "Bed?" She nodded. "Bathroom?" She shook her head. "Eat?" She nodded. Tate chuckled. "Bed and food it is. Do you need some help? Kelly will help you." She nodded, and Kelly came into the room.

"Hi, I'm Kelly," she said.

Teresa nodded, and Kelly helped her get up. Tate didn't move; he closed his eyes when the blanket fell away and waited for Kelly to cover her in the bed.

"Do you want me to stay with you while Tate gets you something to eat?" Kelly asked her. She nodded, watching Tate.

As Tate rose to his six-foot-four-inch height, he noticed Teresa shaking. Tate shook his head. "I know I'm a big guy, but I am not going to hurt you. I promise. You are safe here."

Kelly giggled. "He is just a big old teddy bear."

Tate made his way out of the room, but not before he grabbed the bottle of Jack off the table. Walking into the kitchen, he grabbed his glass and filled it, swallowing it all in one drink. Josh just watched him. Tate nodded and then opened the fridge so he could cook food for Teresa.

Kelly managed to get Teresa to go in the bathroom to clean up. She noticed that Tate put a sheet over the mirror, which she was grateful for. Teresa's face was black and blue, and her hair was matted to her head and full of dirt. It was difficult at best to see what color it was. Kelly thought it might be red, but with all the dirt and dried blood it was hard to tell. She noticed that Teresa winced when she used the toilet, which brought tears to Kelly's eyes.

"Do you want to brush your teeth or anything? Maybe take a shower?"

Teresa shook her head. She hadn't spoken, just kept her eyes as wide open as she could, like a scared rabbit in a cage. Kelly managed to get her back in bed just as Tate knocked on the door.

He walked in with a tray full of food. Teresa didn't take her eyes off him. Tate smiled and said, "I made eggs, sausage, and toast, and I brought you some orange juice and milk. I wasn't sure what you liked. Can I set the tray on the bed?"

Teresa nodded to him. Tate slowly walked to the bed and set the tray down. "If you don't like it, I can make you something else. I'm no good at pancakes." He smiled at her. He noticed when he set the tray down that she was shaking. "I promise, that I am not going to hurt you. You are safe here."

He backed away and watched her. She looked back and forth between the food and Tate. He nodded for her to go ahead and eat. When he got to the door, she reached for the food, grabbing a handful of eggs and stuffing them in her mouth. He felt the tears coming and fought hard to keep them at bay. She was stuffing her face like she was an animal. He knew she had been starved; no woman would ever be that thin on purpose. She watched him like she was expecting him to attack her for eating, so Tate left the room so she would feel comfortable. Walking back into the kitchen, he filled his glass again, swallowing the contents in one gulp.

Josh didn't say a word. He didn't know the whole truth behind Tate's sobriety, but he knew parts of it. Tate opened the cabinet under the sink and pulled out a bucket, putting it in the sink and filling it with cold water. When it was full, he carried it out the door, across the yard, and into the shed. The guys followed him without saying a word. None of them had ever seen him like this. They knew him to be a kind, caring man. As big as he was, none of them ever expected to see this dark side.

The man tied to the chair was still out, so he poured the cold water on him. Tate sat back down in his chair while the man sputtered awake.

"What was she conditioned for?" Tate asked with an even tone.

"You fucking broke my arm, you bastard!" he screamed.

Tate swung the tree branch, clipping him across the knee. The guy flipped backwards, screaming in pain. Josh and Devlin picked him back up.

"What was she conditioned for?"

"To be a submissive," the guy cried.

"A submissive for who?"

"Anyone who wanted her." The guy winced, waiting for Tate to hit him again.

"Who conditioned her?"

"The guy who owned her before I bought her for my client."

Tate swung again, clipping him across the other knee, sending him backwards. He knew the guy was in pain, probably even crying under the hood, but he didn't care. What that woman went through was seared into his brain. Josh and Devlin sat him upright.

"Who conditioned her?"

"I don't know, man. I really don't know. Please," the guy begged.

"Where did you pick her up at?"

"A place in the city called The Black Cat."

Tate looked at Josh; they knew the place. It was Sully's place.

"Do you know who she is?"

"No, they told me her name was Julie."

"Why were you beating her in the street?"

"She went ballistic in the car. She was fucking hitting me and kicking me. Then the bitch fucking bit me."

Tate smiled and swung the branch, connecting with the guy's shoulder. He flew to the floor, slamming his head and knocking himself out. Tate dropped the branch and walked out into the yard.

He felt a sense of pride for her. After everything that had happened to her, she still fought. He looked at the cabin, shaking his head. How scared she must have been, how weak and scared, but she still fought.

Josh walked up behind him. "You okay?" They had been through some shit, him and Tate. Never had he seen him lose his cool like this.

"No, not really. I'm going for a run. I need to clear my head," Tate said and took off running. He ran the trails for a long time. When he arrived back at the cabin, Teresa was asleep, and Kelly was standing guard over her. "I'm going to take a shower," he told her as he quietly gathered his clothes.

"I'll be on the porch. I need to call James and check on him and Taylor."

Tate nodded to his sister and then closed the bathroom door. He showered and got dressed. Sitting himself in the chair he occupied the night before, he stared at Teresa.

How brave she must have been. He knew in his heart that those whip marks were from Frank, but how? How did he survive? Maybe that's why he was never arrested, but why would they not tell him that he was still alive? Tate let his mind go back to that day.

～

He had come home late from football practice, which was the norm for him. He hated going in that house while Frank was home. He knew that coming home late afforded him the peace of not having to sit at the dinner table with him.

When Tate walked in the back door, he panicked. The kitchen table was flipped over, and the dishes were broken. There was food everywhere. Spin-

ning around, he looked at the garage. No, no, no, he thought to himself. He listened carefully to see if he could hear them, but it was silent. Tate slowly walked out the back door toward the garage. As he reached for the handle on the door, he noticed his hand was shaking. Giving himself a mental shake, he turned the knob, pushing the door open. It was dark inside, and he couldn't see anything. Frank had painted the windows black years ago. He reached for the light switch, and when he flipped it on, his heart slammed in his chest.

Swallowing hard, he saw his mother's lifeless body lying on the floor. He could see that her dress was covered in blood across the back. His whole body shook. As he stepped forward, he scanned the room looking for Frank, looking for Kelly, but there was nothing. He knelt next to his mother with tears running down his cheeks and touched her neck to see if there was a pulse. She was still alive. He needed to get help. He needed to find Kelly. Tate stood, and he felt the bite of Frank's whip across his back as it ripped through his jersey, slicing his skin.

"Fucking little bastard," Frank spat at him.

The blind fury that raged through Tate was like nothing he had ever felt. It had been years since Frank whipped him, and he would never flick that whip again. Tate spun around and charged Frank, slamming him against the bench on the back wall, punching him in the face again and again. He had caught Frank off guard. The old man didn't stand a chance.

Tate beat him and beat him, until he fell to the ground, lifeless. Then he kicked him a few times. When he finished, Tate ran to the neighbors, covered in Frank's blood, and asked them to call the police. The neighbor's husband came back to the house with him, and they waited for the police and ambulance to come.

"My sister is gone," Tate said, sitting behind his mother. "I don't know where she is."

The neighbor ran into the house, searching and calling out her name. When he returned, he shook his head. "She's not in the house." As he looked down at Tate's mother, he noticed a foot sticking out from under her dress. "Tate," he whispered.

Tate looked up and then followed the neighbor's gaze. Together, they gently moved his mother, and the neighbor pulled Kelly out from underneath her. She was unconscious as well. When the neighbor picked her up, Tate saw *whip marks on her back. His anger was so intense when he looked at Frank then he got up and grabbed a pipe and beat the shit out of his lifeless body. The neighbor did nothing to stop him. They had heard Frank beat the kids; the whole neighborhood was afraid of him.*

Teresa moved in the bed, snapping Tate from his memory. She winced and then screamed. Tate wanted to run to her side, but he knew she would freak out. She sat up in the bed and looked right at him.

He smiled. "You're safe. No one is going to hurt you again."

Tears fell from her wide eyes as she sat there looking at him.

Kelly was standing in the doorway the whole time, watching her brother. She had her own demons about Frank and what he did to her. Things she believed Tate never knew.

"Do you need anything? Are you in pain? Should I get Kelly?" Teresa shook her head to all of his questions. "You go back to sleep. You are safe now," he reassured her.

Teresa laid back down and went back to sleep. Tate turned to see Kelly standing in the door, and she smiled at him. "You want me to sit with her? You haven't eaten since I got here. Why don't you go eat? I left some food for you in the oven."

Tate nodded to her, and they switched places.

While he was eating, the guys filled him in on what information they had discovered, which wasn't much. The guy in the shed was just a go-between for the supplier and the customers. As much as it sickened Tate to think of it that way, it's exactly the way it was. They needed a plan of action. They needed to become a customer.

"Josh, I think you need to become a buyer. We need to find this bastard who thinks it's acceptable to sell women. The first place to start is at Sully's club, The Black Cat. Do we have any pictures of that fucker?" he asked.

"No, boss, there are none with a clear face," Devlin answered him.

"Well, do we at least have a general description of him?"

"Yeah, he is about six-feet, with brown hair and a medium build, but that's about it."

"All right, Josh, you go and do your thing. Do not come back here. Once you start asking questions, I am sure you will be tailed. Use the penthouse as your place of residence. Make it look like you are rich. You know the routine."

The penthouse was where they hid people, a place that they worked from on certain cases. No one lived there, so it was the perfect spot. The deed was buried in a massive amount of paperwork and would take a year to figure out who owned it out right. Josh left the cabin and the chase began.

"I'm going to chat with our friend in the shed again, but I want to check on the girls first. I'll be right back."

The guys nodded, and Tate went back to the bedroom.

"How's she doing?" he asked Kelly.

"Well, she ate everything you brought her and then threw it all up. Tate, she has been starved. Is it wise to keep her here? She should be in a hospital where they can take care of her."

"I know, but whoever had the balls enough to kidnap an ADA and torture her would be more than willing to end her life. For now, she stays here, until we can figure this shit out. The guys are on it, so hopefully, we can reunite her with her family soon." He looked at Teresa, who was sleeping. "Just keep giving her food, anything she wants. One of the guys will go get it for her. I'll be back in a little while, and then you can go home. But I'm going to need you to come back."

"I already told James I was with a girlfriend who just had a bad break-up with her new boyfriend, so his mom is going to keep Taylor for a few days. I can stay."

"Thanks," Tate said as he walked out of the room. As he moved into the kitchen, he said to one of the guys, "If you find her family, tell them as little as possible. And don't tell them she is alive." He continued out the door and back to the shed.

He pulled the chair right in front of the guy so he was inches from his face. "Tony," he said. The guy pulled his head back. "You do know you are never leaving here, right? That your life is going to end in the darkness of this bag." He reached up and flicked him in the head. "How you choose to leave this planet is up to you. Either you tell me what I want to know, and I will put a bullet in your head, or we can play the game some more and you can suffer until there is no life left. It doesn't matter to me which way we do it. I watched you beat a woman in the street, a woman who has been starved, beaten, raped, and whipped with a whip. No one deserves that."

"She wanted those things. That is what the man who sold her to me told me. He has sold me lots of women, and none of them complained," Tony said.

Tate punched him in the face. "Do you really believe that a woman fighting for her life wants to be beaten? You are one sick mother fucker. I was raised by a sick mother fucker, and you know what, Tony? I killed his fucking ass, too. Who sold you this particular girl?"

"I told you, a guy at The Black Cat in the city."

Tate hit him again. "What is the guy's name?"

"Joe, that's all I know. His fucking name is Joe," Tony said.

"Well, who the fuck does Joe work for, Tony?"

"Man, you are going to get me killed."

"No, Tony, you are already dead. Consider this a cleansing of the soul."

"Fuck!" Tony yelled. "He fucking works for Blake Sully. Fucking Blake Sully sold her to me."

Tate looked up at Devlin and nodded. Devlin pulled out his gun, handing it to him. Tate leaned in to Tony. "The woman you were sold, she was kidnapped six months ago. Her name is Teresa Barns, and she is and Investigative Assistant District Attorney. You know what that means, Tony? It means that transporting her across the state lines is a federal offense. Now, tell me, Tony, before you leave here, who was your client?"

"Fuck! Some guy named Alex Welch. He's a big wig from New York, some kind of stock broker."

Tate stood and put the gun to Tony's head and pulled the trigger. Looking at Devlin, he said, "Take this piece of shit and drop him off at

Sully's." He wiped his prints off the gun, dropping it on the floor. "Then get back here and clean this place up. You're going to New York."

Devlin nodded. this wasn't the first time he had to clean up after Tate. He was the cleaner of the group. The things that they did to protect people called for a cleaner every once in a while. Tate had saved his life a few times, and he owed him. This girl needed to be protected, and Tate had made it his mission.

Tate walked back to the cabin. Josh hadn't checked in yet, so he went in the bedroom to relieve Kelly. "Go get some sleep. I'll stay with her."

"You sure?" Kelly asked.

"Yeah, I'm done for the day. If I need you, I'll send one of the guys in. Has Doc been in?"

"No, he ran back to the city to get some supplies from the shop. He should be back soon."

"Thanks." Tate hugged his sister and she left.

He walked over to the bed to look at Teresa, whispering, "You are safe here with me."

He moved away to sit in the chair, put his head back, and closed his eyes. The only sound he could hear was her breathing. It was her scream that woke him. Jumping up, he moved to the bed. "Shh, you're safe now," he whispered.

Teresa's eyes flew open, and she jumped away from him. He saw her wince in pain.

"It's all right, Teresa. You're safe now," he whispered, his heart breaking at the sight of her. She pulled the covers around her. "Maybe if you had some clothes to put on you would feel better." He got up slowly and walked over to the dresser, pulling out a pair of sweats and a t-shirt. He went back to the bed and set them down. Chuckling, he said, "I'm sure they'll be too big for you, but go ahead and put them on." He turned around so she would feel comfortable.

He heard the sheet move, and he smiled. What woman would feel comfortable with a strange man? Not many. He waited a few minutes and then turned around and smiled when he saw she was dressed.

"Better?" he asked. She nodded at him. "Can I get you something to eat? I didn't finish all the food Kelly made for me. I can warm it up for you." She nodded again. "Be right back." He went to the kitchen and grabbed the plate out of the warmer, grabbed some silverware and a napkin, and poured a glass of milk. He put everything on a tray and took it back to the bedroom.

When he walked in, she was gone. Panic filled his heart, but then he heard the toilet flush, and he relaxed. He put the tray on the table and sat in the chair to wait. When she came out, he rose and waited for her to get back into bed, then he set the tray down for her. "It's mac and cheese, my favorite. Kelly makes the best mac and cheese on the planet." He went back over and sat in the chair.

He tried not to watch her eat, but he couldn't help it. She used the spoon this time instead of her hands and took her time. He didn't speak to her while she ate. When she finished, he got up and took the tray back to the kitchen. Returning, he quietly shut the door and went back to his seat. Teresa was lying down under the covers. Tate turned off the light, put his head back, and closed his eyes.

"Thank you," she said in a soft whisper.

Tate smiled and raised his head. "There is no need to thank me."

He heard her sniffle. If there's one thing that could bring Tate Miles to his knees, it's a woman crying. He got up and walked over to the bed. Slowly sitting down, he whispered, "I can't imagine how scared you are. Please, just know that you are safe now. You can heal, and as soon as I stop the sick bastard that did this to you, I will take you home to your family."

She nodded.

He got up to go back to his chair, and she reached out and touched his hand. "Will you hold me? I'm so scared."

She didn't have to ask him twice. He kicked off his shoes and climbed in the bed next to her. She moved slowly into the crook of his arm, and he gently wrapped his arm around her, trying not to put too much pressure on her back.

"I've got you," he whispered. She was crying; he could feel her tears soaking his shirt. "You're safe. No one is going to hurt you."

Eventually, she calmed down and fell asleep. Tate slept but not like he needed to sleep. He heard Kelly come in and then go out again. Tate didn't bother to open his eyes. He waited until Teresa woke. She didn't move, but her breathing changed so he knew she was awake. She turned her head and looked up at him, then pulled away and sat up.

"Thank you," she whispered, turning her head away from him.

He chuckled. "Anytime," he whispered. "Doc will want to check you out this morning, and Kelly probably has some breakfast going, so I will leave you to it." He swung his legs over the side of the bed. It was when she touched his back that he froze. The gentle, kind gesture sent a strange sensation through his body. He turned to look at her. Her face may have been black and blue, her lips may have been swollen, but her eyes were warm.

"His name is Blake Sully," she whispered.

Tate felt her hand shake. "I know," he said. "He will pay for this." He got up and left her sitting on the bed.

In the kitchen, Kelly gave him a look. "Really, Tate?"

He smiled at her. "What?"

"The woman has been through hell, and you made a move on her?"

Tate busted out laughing and hugged her. "Little sister, I hope to God you know me better than that. The lady asked me to hold her. Who am I to argue with that?"

She smacked him in the chest. "Oh, I am so sure it was a struggle. Remember, she is a victim."

"Kelly, you don't need to remind me of anything. What's for breakfast?"

"I swear you only have me out here to feed your big ass." She laughed. "I made pancakes. The guys already ate. Yours are in the warmer, and these are for Teresa." She picked up the tray and went to the bedroom.

Tate grabbed his pancakes and sat at the table. "So, what's going on?"

"Well, Dev is on his way to New York, and so far, we haven't heard anything from Josh."

"I want everything you've got on Sully, everything you can find out about his life, his past. Hell, I want to know where that fucker was born," Tate said.

"Strange thing with that, everything we have on him ends like fifteen years ago. Before then, it's like he never existed."

Tate stopped chewing and slowly picked his head up. "What do you mean?" He swallowed hard. It was as if ice replaced the warm blood flowing through his veins.

"Just what I said. Blake Sully didn't exist past fifteen years ago. There is nothing."

With a shaky breath, Tate said, "I want everything you have on him. Steve, get to the city and make contact with Josh. Find out what is going on."

"Will do, boss."

Tate put his plate in the sink then walked into the bedroom. "I need to run," he said to Kelly. "Stay here with her while Doc looks her over. He is going to need some help cleaning her back. I'll be back when I'm done." Picking up his shoes, he walked out of the room and out onto the porch. Sitting on the bench, he put his shoes on and took off.

Running was something Tate loved to do. It was the only place he really felt free, especially if he was running over ragged terrain. His mind needed to concentrate on the here and now so he didn't break his neck. He pounded the miles, but his mind was occupied on Sully. Was it possible at all that he was the same man? He had connections at the PD, but this woman was an ADA. If she went missing and no one did anything about it, then Sully could own the PD. He figured it was best to keep it at home for now.

He thought back, remembering if he heard anything about her disappearance. Shaking his head, he stopped and pulled out his phone to call Manny.

"Hey, I need a favor. Find out everything there is about Teresa Barns, and I mean everything."

He hung up and kept running. He didn't want to invade her privacy, but something didn't feel right about this. If she was his girlfriend, and she went missing, he would have used the entire Chicago police department to try to find her. He headed back to the cabin. Tate had been out running for almost two hours. When he walked in, Manny had gathered a great deal of information.

"Let me grab a shower first," Tate said to him and set the folder down. He made his way into the bedroom. "Hey, I am going to jump in the shower."

Kelly nodded. "Doc cleaned her up. It was bad, Tate. She's been sleeping for a while. I am going to make some lunch."

"Thanks, Kelly." She smiled at him and left the room. He grabbed a pair of jeans and a t-shirt out of the closet and then a pair of boxers and headed to the bathroom. He reached in and turned on the water and then lifted his shirt off his back.

Teresa had opened her eyes just as his scars came into view. She held her breath as he lowered his sweats and boxers, exposing more scars. "Uh," she breathed out.

Tate turned and looked at her then reached up and gently closed the door. Closing his eyes, he shook his head. It was not his intention to get naked in front of this woman who had obviously been brutalized sexually. He took his shower and got dressed. His hand hesitated on the door knob, but when he opened it, her eyes were closed. Tate walked to the bed and moved her hair off her face, whispering, "I'm sorry, didn't mean to scare you."

He was halfway to the door when he heard her small voice. "It happened to you, too." It wasn't a question; it was a statement. Tate froze. He often forgot about his scars. That is what she was talking about.

He dropped his head, nodding, and continued out the door. Kelly met him in the hall with a tray for Teresa. "You all right?" she asked.

He smiled and kissed her on the forehead. "I will be."

Kelly went in the bedroom, and Tate went to have a drink and talk to Manny. "So, what do we know?" he said, pouring his drink.

Manny just looked at him. They all knew he didn't drink anymore. It was just too much for him to deal with right now. But he would get through it any way he could.

"Well, Sully…" he started.

Tate held up his hand. "Let's start with Teresa."

Manny nodded and picked up a different file. "She was born on July 29th 1988, to Martha and James Barns in Evergreen Park, Ill. Her father worked on the railroad, some big wig, while her mother was a stay at home mom. She has two sisters and a brother. She graduated from Harvard with a Master's degree in Criminal Justice. She is the youngest Investigative Assistant DA that Chicago has ever seen. Her boyfriend is Detective Theodore Hardt of the Chicago PD. She went missing from the courthouse on January 8th, just before a Grand Jury hearing. The initial investigation into her disappearance scouted foul play, but after word got out about her not so good relationship, Hardt told people that she left him and he was too embarrassed to say anything. He claimed she must have moved away. Her parents and family don't believe him. They have been trying to get the PD to charge him with her murder. But, they said that without a body, they did not want to ruin his much-decorated career."

Tate looked at him. "I want everything you can find on him. Get a tail on him. Seems to me he might be into this cover-up deeper than anyone thinks."

"Tate, man, we're talking about a decorated cop here. If we are wrong, it will be over for us."

"I don't give a fuck. If he is a bad cop, then he is a bad cop. We work with the fucking cops in this city, and if one is bad, there have to be others. I am so fucking sick of the cover-ups we deal with. Find everything. Is there any word from Josh and Devlin?"

"Nothing yet, I will let you know as soon as someone checks in."

"Thanks." Tate picked up the files and went back to the bedroom. Kelly was just getting everything picked up. He dropped in the chair, setting the files on the table along with his drink.

Kelly walked by. "Should you be drinking that?"

Tate chuckled. "Yeah, I'm fine, and thank you."

She bent and kissed his head. He wrapped his arms around her waist and put his head on her stomach, hugging her. Kelly left, pulling the door closed behind her.

Tate looked at Teresa, who was sitting in the bed with her legs drawn up to her chest.

"I'm sorry," she whispered.

"What are you sorry for?"

"For stepping out of line and questioning you."

Tate closed his eyes. Fucking Sully had diminished her. He shook his head. "You can ask me anything you want. There is no need to apologize for being curious." He put his head back and closed his eyes. "It was a lifetime ago," he whispered.

"Was it him?" she whispered, her eyes wide with fear.

"I don't even know who he is." He wanted to see how far he could push her to talk. She was the one who'd been there. She would know more than he could ever find on his own.

"Blake Sully," she whispered. "He did this to me."

Tate swallowed hard. He picked up his glass and drank the contents. "I am so sorry for what happened to you. I will make sure he pays with his life."

"You do know who I am, right?" Her voice was getting a bit louder.

Tate chuckled. "You're an ADA. I know everything there is to know about you." Tate looked at her now, taking in her eyes, huge and full of fear. "I just got the file," he added and picked it up.

"How? Who are you?"

"I own a private security office. I secure things and people."

"Am I secure here?" she questioned him.

Tate smiled. "If you are asking me if you are safe, then yes. No one will get to you while you are with me. If you are asking if you are a prisoner here, the answer is no. You are free to go whenever you want."

"Oh," she said, looking at him.

"You have information I am going to need to help you. That is, if you want my help."

She didn't say anything for a long time; she just sat there looking at him and him at her. Finally, she said, "I'm not sure I can talk about it."

"I don't want you to. I want you to tell me about where you were, some of the things he said to you. Why he took you, how he was able to get to you. It says you disappeared from the courthouse downtown. How did they get you out of a secure building without raising any suspicion? This wasn't just Sully's doing. Someone, a bunch of some-one's helped him. That's what I want to know. The rest of it, I don't need to know. If you need someone to talk to, I am here. Kelly's here. That's why I asked her to come."

"Is she your girlfriend? Your wife?" She was embarrassed.

Tate smiled. "No, Teresa, she is my little sister." She nodded and laid down. Tate went about reading his files. When he finished, he turned off the light and put his head back, closing his eyes. He hadn't been asleep long when her screams woke him. Jumping up, he was at the bedside instantly. Kelly came running in. "Shh, you are safe," he said to her.

She sat up, opening her eyes wide, and scurried to the other side of the bed. Her eyes darted from him to Kelly then back again. "If you'd like, Kelly can stay with you, and I can go sleep out there."

She shook her head. Kelly smiled. "I'm here if you need me," she said as she left.

Tate got up to go back to the chair when he heard her whisper silently, "Stay with me." He wasn't sure he heard her.

When he turned around, she was crying. It took two strides before he was in the bed next to her. Her whole body shook as she curled up next to him. After she calmed down, she said. "I will tell you every-thing I can remember under one condition."

"What would that be?"

"That you let me be there when you kill him."

Tate didn't say anything; he just closed his eyes and held her. It was Kelly that woke him.

"Hey," she whispered as she touched his chest. Tate opened his eyes. "The guys have checked in, and Manny needs you."

He nodded and worked his way out of bed, trying not to disturb Teresa. Then he followed Kelly into the kitchen.

"What's up?"

Manny looked up when he heard Tate's voice. "Well, Josh made contact, and he needs to talk to you. He said to meet him at the pent-house as soon as you can get there. Dev has his eyes on Welch. Apparently, this guy is the head of some Investment Brokerage House. He has all kinds of money and all kinds of connections."

"Yeah, I really don't give a fuck about who he is connected to. Get in touch with Josh and tell him I'll be there in about an hour. I'll call Dev on my way into the city." He looked at Doc. "Make sure she is comfortable and don't give her any information yet."

Turning, he looked at Kelly. She said to him, "Can we talk before you go?" He nodded and she walked outside. "What are you doing, Tate?"

"I am going to find out who this bastard is."

"No not with Sully, with Teresa. She has been through a horrible experience."

He smiled. "She asked me to hold her. She was crying and upset."

She smiled. "And you can't resist a woman in tears. Tate, be careful. She is damaged goods. I just don't want to see you get hurt. It's been a long time since you've been with someone."

He laughed. "Little sister, not that it's any of your business, but I am not a saint. Just because you haven't met any of the women I've been involved with doesn't mean there aren't any. You know me better. I'm a man of honor, and never once have I crossed the line with a client."

"Yeah, Tate, except she is not a client of her own free will. You have taken this on as a personal issue, and we both know why. I'm just looking out for you. I won't ever forget what she did to you, even if you think you can."

That stung Tate. He was still bitter, that wound still fresh. He hugged her. "Don't worry, baby girl. I'm fine. I need to get going. Take care of her."

"I will. When will you be back?"

"I shouldn't be too long." He let her go and went back in the house to shower and change.

This time, when he went in the bathroom, he closed the door. He was showered and dressed in ten minutes. When he walked out,

Teresa was looking at him. He sat on the edge of the bed and moved a piece of her hair behind her ear. "I have to go into the city. The guys here will keep you safe. Kelly is here, and remember, no one knows where you are."

"I need some clean clothes and personal things," she said in a small voice.

"How about you and Kelly make a list, and when I get back, she can go shopping for you and get what you need. We are going to need more food anyway."

She nodded and touched his arm. "Thank you."

"There is no need to thank me. I will see you in a few hours." Getting up, he grabbed the files and walked to the door, then turned to look at her. "It will be fine. Don't worry, you are safe here."

She half-smiled at him and laid down, pulling the covers over her.

In the kitchen, he said to Kelly, "Talk to Teresa. She is going to need some things, and when I get back, I am going to need you to go shopping."

"Yeah, I was going to suggest it. We're going to need food and stuff. I have enough to put something in the crock pot, so there will be dinner when you get back. Tate?" He turned to look at her. "Please, be careful."

He chuckled and kissed her on the forehead, "Always am."

Tate left and started the drive back to the city. He called Devlin. "Hey, man, what's up?"

"Well, I found the guy. He's some kind of big shot here. I've set up to listen in on his phone conversations, and right now, I'm waiting to follow him home so I can wire his house. Tate, are you sure about this? I mean, this is huge."

"He isn't who we're after, but if we can shut him down along with the rest of these fuckers, then it's an added bonus. What we need is to link him to this fucked up situation and cut the head off the fucking snake. These guys are buying and selling women, Dev, and as a man, I can't live with myself knowing this is happening when I can do something about it."

"Yeah, I get it. Once your face is shoved in the pie, you have a hard time not licking off the filling. Knowing it's happening is one thing, but having it in front of your face is another. I'll check in when I have more to tell you."

"Thanks Dev. You know what I think?"

He chuckled. "No, man, I don't think anyone knows what you think."

Tate laughed. "I think, when this is over, we all need a vacation."

"Agreed. I'll talk to you later." He hung up.

Tate's drive to the city felt quick to him. Before he knew it, he was pulling into the underground garage of the Legacy in downtown Chicago. As for the routine, he took the elevator to the sixtieth floor and then took the stairs up to the penthouse. He was the only one who had the keys to open the door that led into the hallway. As he walked in, he remembered why he bought this place. He hoped one day to retire here. The views were spectacular from the floor to ceiling windows.

"Anybody home?" he called out as he went in.

There was no answer, so he walked around the place, checking to see if anyone was here. As he made his way into the master bedroom, he couldn't help but feel something wasn't right. Looking at the bed, he realized that it hadn't been slept in, which was strange because Josh was supposed to act like he was living here. He'd been here for two days now. As he moved through the room, he realized that the bathroom light was on so he headed that way. As he pushed the door open, fear welled up inside of him.

"Fuck," he whispered as the scene unfolded with each movement of the door. Josh was strung up in the shower, his back sliced open from a whip. Tate pulled his phone out of his pocket and dialed nine-one-one. "I'm in the penthouse on the seventy-second floor of The Legacy. There is a man dead here. Please send an ambulance." He hung up. "Fuck," he whispered as he moved closer to him. Stepping into the shower, he noticed there was no blood, so he came around to the front of Josh's body. Reaching up, he felt for a pulse, knowing damn well there would be none. "I'm so sorry, buddy," he whispered, touching his face. Tate moved out of the shower and pulled his gun, moving through the apartment, looking for whoever did this.

His phone vibrated in his pocket, scaring the shit out of him. He fished it out, but the number was unknown. He accepted the call without saying anything.

"I believe you have something that belongs to me. I want it back."

Tate froze as a memory flashed in his mind.

~

He was sixteen again, rummaging through the cabinet in the kitchen, looking for something to eat. Frank never let them have anything but dinner, and he was so hungry. He found some cookies hidden behind some cans of vegetables and ate some. He went to bed, and in the middle of the night, his bedroom door flew open and Frank grabbed him out of bed. He threw him to the floor and kicked him in the ribs. He grabbed him by the neck, pulling him up, and said in his ear, "I believe you took something that belongs to me, and I want them back."

~

Tate's hand was shaking. There was no fucking way he survived. No fucking way is Frank and Blake Sully one and the same. Although, he already suspected it, now, he knew for a fact.

"Come and get it, fucker," he said into the phone and then hung up. He walked into the kitchen, dropped his phone into the garbage disposal, and turned it on. He made his way out the back door and down the stairs to the parking garage. Instead of getting in his car, he walked out onto the street and grabbed a cab. The police were coming, flying down the street. There was no place that was safe right now. If Sully knew it was him, he would have someone tailing him.

He had the cabby drop him off at the Apple store and he got a new phone. He called Manny. "Shut it down and get them out now and get rid of Kelly's car. I'll meet you at the drop." He hung up. Walking out onto the street, he grabbed another cab and headed to the airport. The cab dropped him off, and he went inside like he was leaving but headed to the underground walkway and into the parking structure. He had a Range Rover in long term parking there. He picked it up, paid the bill, and headed out of the city.

Tate made sure there was no one following him. He drove out of the city and headed to Arlington. As he drove, he could think of nothing but Frank, aka Blake Sully. The more he thought, the more he realized that there was no way he could've known it was him. Not unless Josh gave him up, but that's just something Josh wouldn't do. When he was captured and tortured, Josh didn't give anything up. Tate grabbed the phone and called Manny.

"Are you out?" He asked.

"Yeah, we dumped Kelly's car in the lake. Man, she is pissed."

Tate chuckled. "I'll buy her a new one."

"You are buying me a new car, Tate," he heard Kelly yell in the background.

"Listen, meet me in Arlington," Tate said.

"We are just about there, what's going on?"

"Josh is gone," Tate said softly.

"Got it, see you there." Manny hung up and threw his phone out the window. He took Kelly's and Doc's, pitching them as well.

When Tate pulled up to the estate and its surrounding ten acres of land, the place looked abandoned. He opened one of the garage doors and pulled in. As he got out, he could see that every bay in the six-car garage was full. This was one of those times when he was glad he could just walk into the house without having to go outside. He needed to make sure she was safe, that they were safe. Frank could not get to Kelly or Teresa again. He knew without a doubt that he would inflict the same punishment on Kelly, and that he would take up right where he left off all those years ago. Their mother had given her life to save Kelly from being raped by that asshole.

When he walked into the kitchen, Kelly and Doc were waiting for him.

"What happened?" Doc asked.

"I got to the penthouse, and he was strung up in the shower. I called the police, and a few minutes later, Sully called me on my phone. So, I am thinking that he has people in the police department. My phone was a burner phone, so I dropped it in the garbage disposal and got the hell out of there." Tate looked at Kelly.

"What aren't you telling us, Tate?" she asked quietly, knowing what the answer was but not wanting to know it just the same.

"I'm not telling you that I believe Blake Sully is in fact Frank James." Tate watched as his sister processed what he said. He saw her eyes change, and he was moving toward her. He wrapped his arms around her while she shook and cried, while she dealt with the memories they both managed to bury deep inside.

"How can this be?" she whispered.

"I don't know, but something is not right here. I need to talk to Teresa. Where is she?"

"She's up in your room."

Tate let her go and looked at Doc. "Is she all right?"

"Yeah, she's coming along, starting to heal. No sign of infection."

"Good, you guys get some rest. Where is Manny?"

"They're setting things up in the office," Kelly said.

"All right, I'm going to stop and see him, and then I am headed up stairs. It's time Teresa and I have a talk."

They both nodded at him. Tate left and made his way to the office. He didn't speak to any one person but to the room.

"I need you guys to set up a perimeter. Get some cameras out there, some motion detectors. I want this place sealed up like Fort Knox. No one gets in. Make sure there are weapons everywhere and show Kelly where the tunnel is and the safe room. She is not to get in this fight. I have some things I need to do, and then we are going to get a battle plan going. Josh is gone, and I think Dev will be next. No one leaves. We have enough food in cold storage and in the freezer to last a month."

They all nodded, and Tate left, heading up to his bedroom. His heart hurt knowing his friend was gone. Everything they had been through and now fucking Frank ended him.

CHAPTER FOUR

He was quiet as he entered the huge master bedroom. Teresa looked so small in the massive king bed. She was curled up in the corner asleep. Tate made his way into the closet and peeled off his clothes. He was standing in his boxer briefs, reaching for a clean t-shirt, when he saw her out of the corner of his eye. He didn't move. She was looking at his back and his thighs, looking at his scars. He saw her move slowly toward him.

Her hand shaking, she reached up and touched his back. "Who did this to you?" Her voice was hardly a whisper.

Tate swallowed hard. "A man my mother married."

"I'm sorry," she said.

Tate reached for his shirt and pulled it over his head. Then he grabbed a pair of sweats and pulled them on. Turning, he looked at her. "There is no need to be sorry. It was a long time ago, and I killed the bastard."

She looked at him. "You don't believe that, do you?" Her voice was so soft, as if she didn't want to say it out loud.

He stared at her. Reaching up, he tucked her hair behind her ear. "No," he whispered and walked out of the closet and back into the bedroom. Tate picked up the file he laid on the dresser and sat down at the table. Teresa came out and climbed on the bed.

"Why are you doing this? You don't even know me," she asked.

Tate turned to look at her. "I was doing the right thing by stopping to help you. When I brought you to the cabin, and Doc rolled you over, I saw your back and it became personal for me."

"Did anyone look for me?" she whispered.

"Your family hasn't stopped, but the police have decided that you ran away."

"He was there with Sully. He watched what he did to me." She reached up to wipe a tear from her cheek.

Tate had to fight the urge to get up and go to her. He had to keep it professional. "Ted?"

Teresa nodded. "He laughed while he watched Sully rape me."

"You don't need to tell me what happened to you. It's obvious you were brutalized. Honestly, I don't want you to relive what he did." Tate tried to be as gentle as possible with his words. He didn't want to know the extent of what happened to her; he could imagine enough. He just needed to get through this, without going to her and holding her in his arms. He had seen pictures of her. He knew how beautiful she was under the swollen face and the black and blue bruises that covered her body. He hadn't been close to a woman on an emotional level in many years, and he didn't want to start now.

"I'm sorry, I'm just feeling a bit sorry for myself." She wiped her face and straightened her back.

Tate sat and watched her transform from the broken woman before him to the hardcore lawyer she once was. She took a deep breath.

"That's it, get pissed off. Take back your life; otherwise, they will beat you. They will win," he said softly.

She nodded. "I need to take a shower. I need to feel human before we start this. Do you think the Doc could take this I.V. out?"

Tate smiled at her, picking up his walkie talkie. "Doc, I need you up here." He set it down on the table then got up and went to the closet. "My sister has some clothes in here. I'm sure they will fit you better than mine will. I can't help you with the under garments, but at least you will have something to put on." He rummaged through a few drawers and came out of the closet with a few pairs of jeans, some shirts, and a few pairs of shorts. "Whatever you need I will try to get for you. But we are locked down for now. Sully killed my best man, and I have a guy in New York watching the man you were being sold to. No one leaves here, not until we have a plan."

She climbed off the bed, touching his arm. "I'm sorry about your friend and thank you for saving me."

He looked at her hand on his arm and then looked at her. This was the first time he saw her eyes, and he noticed they were steel gray with a blue hue. He smiled and nodded at her. "I'll get Kelly so she can help you."

Turning, he went to walk away, and Doc walked in. "What's up?"

"Teresa wants to take a shower. Can I get you to take out her I.V.?"

"That wouldn't be a good idea. I can disconnect it, and then we can cover it so it doesn't get wet. You need those fluids and antibiotics for at least a week," Doc said, looking at Teresa.

Tate walked out the door and let out the breath he was holding. She shook him to his core. What she must have endured by the hands of that fucking mad man. But she was strong. Taking a deep breath, he continued down stairs to find Kelly in the kitchen. "Can you go up and help her? She wants to take a shower."

"You all right?" she asked him.

He leaned in and pulled her into a hug. "I don't think I am ever going to be all right again. I thought I killed the fucker, Kel. It's him. He has been doing this to women for fifteen years."

She squeezed her arms around his waist. "It can't be him, Tate. It just can't be." She pulled away from him and put her hand on his cheek. "I love you," she whispered and walked away.

Doc had finished wrapping Teresa's arm when Kelly walked in. "Tate said you wanted to take a shower?"

Doc looked at her. "When you wash her back, use this. It's a special soap." He handed Kelly a bottle of liquid.

"Thanks, Doc," she said and then leaned in to whisper to him. "Will you check on Tate? He isn't doing so well?"

Doc nodded and smiled at her. "I'll leave you ladies to it."

Once the doc left, Kelly helped Teresa take off her clothes and then get in the shower. "I'm not sure I can wash my hair," she said to Kelly.

"No problem. I'll just get in with you." Kelly smiled as she started to undress. She left her bra and panties on.

Teresa saw the scars across her back. She didn't mean to touch her, but her hand came up and she touched her back. "It happened to you, too?"

Kelly froze when she felt her fingers run along the scars. "And I survived, just like you will." She slowly turned around to see Teresa wipe her tears away. "Hey, you are alive, and my brother is going to help you. It will take time for the dreams to leave, but eventually, you will heal," she said as softly as she could.

"No man is ever going to want me." Teresa was in a near meltdown.

"That's not true. I am married, and I have a beautiful daughter. There is someone out there who will see beyond the scars, beyond the pain. You will know love. Come on, let's get you cleaned up and feeling human again."

Teresa nodded and they got in the shower. Kelly used two palms full of conditioner in her hair. As the water ran through it, rinsing it out, she was surprised to see how long it was. "Let me grab a comb. It might be easier to comb this out in here, then we can wash it again."

As they stood there combing out the mess that was her hair, Kelly counted the whip marks. There we eighteen in all. She herself had five, and Tate had at least twenty-five. He took most of the whippings when they were children. Teresa's were far deeper than hers or Tate's. Kelly thought it was because she and her brother had always had clothes on.

"I'm really sorry this happened to you," Kelly said softly.

"I had to learn to close my mind when he would come at me. I think I made it worse for myself because I kept fighting him."

"Don't say that. It's good that you fought. You got away, and Tate will make sure nothing else happens to you." She had finished combing out her hair. "There, your hair is tangle free. Let's wash it again to get all this cream rinse out, and then I want to do your back again just to be safe." When Teresa's back was thoroughly cleaned, Kelly got out and dried off. She picked up her clothes and said, "I'm going to go to my room and change. I'll be back in a few minutes."

"Thanks, but I should be all right. You don't need to come back."

"You sure?"

Teresa nodded, and Kelly left. She met Tate in the hall. "She has eighteen marks across her back, Tate. They are deep. She is still in the shower."

"Thanks, Kelly, for helping her."

Kelly touched her brother's arm. "Be careful, Tate. She is damaged like we were. Be watchful of your heart."

He smiled at her and walked toward his room. He knocked, but there was no answer so he opened the door and went in. He could hear the water running, so he figured she was still in the shower. Walking over to the table, he opened the file and started reading about her career and her case against Sully. Her boyfriend, Ted Hardt, was a bad cop. They would have to be careful. Tate still had contacts in Washington, but would it be wise to drag them into this mess? It all hinged on Teresa.

He looked at the bathroom door, realizing the water was still running. He got up and walked over to the door, listening. He thought he heard sobbing so he knocked.

"Teresa?" he said into the door. There was no answer. He reached for the knob and turned it. Pushing the door open, he found her with her back to him, curled up in the corner on the floor of the shower.

He didn't have a clue how anyone could survive what she had been through. Doc had filled him in on the extent of her injuries. She had been brutalized sexually, both vaginal and anal, with tears in both places. She had bite marks on her inner thighs, cracked ribs, and a cracked jaw. Her injuries warranted a hospital stay. He just couldn't bring himself to risk her becoming the victim of that fucking monster again. He took off his shoes and socks and reached in, turning off the shower. Then he grabbed the robe on the back of the door and wrapped her in it, gently lifting her off the floor.

"I've got you, beautiful," he said so softly. She buried her head in his neck and cried. He carried her to the bed and laid her down, covering her up. He went to walk away, but she touched his hand. He stopped. She wrapped her tiny hand in his and gave a tiny tug on it. Against his better judgement, he climbed in bed with her and wrapped his arms around her while she cried herself to sleep.

Tate fell asleep, only to be woken by Doc, who was hooking up her I.V. "You all right?" Doc whispered to him. Tate shook his head. Doc nodded and left just as quietly as he came in. Tate closed his eyes and went back to sleep.

He was moving in slow motion toward the garage. There was no sound, nothing, not even his footsteps. As his hand reached for the door knob, he realized his heartbeat was the only sound. Turning the knob and pushing on the door, there was no creaking sound. The room was dark, black as the night sky with no stars. Slowly, he stepped over the threshold into the darkness. The light from the day was leaving. He could make out something on the floor in the middle of the room. As he moved closer, he still could only hear his heartbeat. It was getting faster and louder, echoing off the barren walls. The shape on the floor came into view, and he could vaguely make out a body. Holding his breath, he tried to focus his eyes on it. It was his mother. She wasn't moving. She was covered in blood. Then the crack of the whip echoed in his ears, and that familiar burn sliced through him.

Tate's eyes flew open and he sat up, gasping for air. He had lost control of his dreams. They were back. As his body calmed down, he looked next to him and saw Teresa sleeping. Shaking his head, he got up and went into the bathroom to splash water on his face. Looking in the mirror, he said, "Fuck." He grabbed a towel and wiped off his face. He made his way downstairs to the kitchen. Kelly and Doc were sitting at the table drinking coffee.

Kelly looked at him. "Tate, we need to talk about what is happening."

He smiled at her. "I know. I can feel it, too. I just had a fucking dream again." Shaking his head, he poured a cup of coffee. "I can't walk away now. No matter what happens to me, Kel, I need to stop him."

"I know, and I am right here with you. I'm just afraid you are going to get lost again. I need you. Taylor needs you."

"I can do this. I have to protect you and Taylor. When he figures out it's me, he will come after you just to get to me. I think we should get Taylor here. We have the safe room and the tunnel. She would be safer here than with James."

"I have to agree with you. If anything happened to her, I don't think I would survive it. Doc already said he would go get her."

"Yeah, that isn't going to happen. I can't take that chance. I will go. She'll come with me. She doesn't know Doc that well, and James' mother isn't going to let her go with him. Can you call James and tell him I'll pick her up from school today?"

Kelly nodded and got up. She took his phone, dialing as she walked out of the room.

"Tate," Doc said.

"Yeah, I know. If I need help, I will ask this time. I can't fuck this up."

Doc nodded at him. Kelly walked in the room. "James said all right. I called the school and told them you were coming. There is a back door that you can get to from a street behind the school. You should probably go that way just in case someone is watching."

"Good idea. I'll leave now. I'm just going to talk to the guys." He squeezed her arm as he took his coffee to the office where the guys were.

"Talk to me. Has anyone heard from Dev?" he asked the room.

Manny spoke. "Yeah, he got into the guy's house and wired it. He checked in about half an hour ago. I've been scanning the police bands, and there has been nothing about Josh. You okay?"

"Yeah, did you guys wire this place?"

Manny nodded. "Nothing's getting in here undetected. All the monitors are live."

"Good, I'm heading out to get Taylor. I'll bring her back through the tunnel. I am taking the Jeep. Its low-jacked, so keep an eye on me. If you see anything out of the ordinary, I'm going to need a diversion to get her here. I should be there and back in an hour, maybe an hour and a half. Keep my sister safe, and Teresa as well. She is the only witness to what Sully is doing. All costs, guys." Tate nodded at them and left to get changed. He knew taking the Jeep was the only option. It was armor enforced and had bullet proof glass. It was the safest vehicle.

When he walked into his room, Teresa was sitting on the bed with Kelly eating some pancakes. Tate smiled at them and went to the closet to change. Walking back out into the room, he looked at Kelly. "I'll be back soon."

"Be careful, Tate," she said.

He nodded and left. He stopped off at a clothing store and bought Taylor a bunch of new clothes, picking out an outfit to wear back to the house. He also bought her a doll house with all the furniture and dolls, a late birthday present and something for her to play with while they were hiding out. He made sure he had the best car seat for her. While he was shopping, he picked up some things for Teresa as well, guessing at her size. The women in the store helped him with the panties and bras. It was a bit uncomfortable for him, buying such intimate things for a woman he didn't know. But he managed.

Then he headed to Taylor's school. When he got there, he checked the place out, but there didn't seem to be anything out of the ordinary. Hopefully, Sully had no clue who he was yet. He walked in the back way like Kelly told him and went to the office. Taylor was waiting for him. She ran up and gave him a hug.

"Hey, sweetheart, let's leave your backpack and stuff here for now. I brought the Jeep," he told her.

Her smile said it all. She loved to ride in the jeep. Tate wasn't sure if she was carrying a transmitter or not. He wouldn't put it past Sully, especially if he thought it was him coming after him. "I bought you some new clothes to wear in case we decided to get dirty. I wouldn't want your pretty clothes to get ruined." He helped her change right there in the office in front of the ladies who worked there. Tate folded her pretty dress and put everything in her backpack. He'd even bought her new boots to wear.

He handed the backpack to the receptionist. "Can we leave this here? Her mom will pick it up tomorrow." The woman just sat there nodding and smiling at him. He smiled back and thanked her.

"You ready, sweetheart?" he asked Taylor. She nodded with a huge smile on her face. They made their way through the school and out the back door. Tate was hyper aware of his surroundings. He was with the single most important person in his life. Just the thought of Sully touching her or even getting close enough to her made the blood in his veins turn to ice. They made it to the Jeep with no incident. Taylor was so excited to see her new doll house. He scanned the Jeep to make sure it was clean then smiled. He loved his gadgets.

Once Tate got Taylor and himself settled in the Jeep, he let out a breath he didn't know he was holding. At least, inside, she was safe from bullets. They started the trip back to the house. Tate made sure no one was following them; he went through the woods off the road and came to the entrance to the tunnel. He pressed the garage door opener, and the earth opened up. After they drove through, he stopped to make sure the doors closed without incident.

When they emerged from the tunnel, Kelly was waiting for them. Looking at Tate as she wrapped her arms around Taylor, she said, "You've been gone for a long time. I was getting worried. Did every-thing go all right?"

He smiled at her, but Taylor interrupted him before he could speak. "Mommy, Uncle Tay got me a doll house."

"Did he now?"

She nodded. "For my birthday."

Kelly looked up at Tate. "Is that right?"

Tate laughed, looking past her to Manny. "Hey, man, can you give me a hand?"

Manny nodded, and they headed back down to where he'd parked. It took two loads to get everything. They carried it upstairs to Taylor and Kelly's room. He grabbed the bags of things he had bought for Teresa and went to his room. It was time for him and Teresa to talk.

He made sure he knocked before he entered. Teresa was sleeping, so he went in and changed his clothes, putting back on his sweats. He looked at himself in the mirror. The rage that pumped through his body wasn't obvious to anyone but him. The horrors that stayed just below the surface of his consciousness scared the shit out of him. It's what drove him to be who he is. Unfeeling to pain, capable of murder, guilty of murder and many other crimes. He let one woman into his world, into his life. She promised him that she loved him enough to know the truth of why he was incapable of giving himself completely to anyone. He gave her all he could give, and she still wanted more. She wanted it all. He trusted her enough to let her in, and she left him when he shared with her the truth.

Shaking his head, he whispered to his reflection, "Never again." He saw her move behind him. As he looked at her reflection in the mirror, their eyes met. She saw him; she saw deep inside him to the raw emotion he let no one see. He turned to look at her. Teresa didn't waver in her stance. Her hair was combed out and clean. It was a remarkable deep red and came nearly to her waist, which wasn't saying much since she only stood about five feet maybe 5 inches tall.

She swallowed under his gaze. "You all right?"

His lips curved up just enough to keep up the lie he'd been living for fifteen years. "I bought you some things. I wasn't sure of the size of most of it, but I thought you would like to have a few things that were your own. At least, until you can go back home to your family."

He walked past her out into the bedroom, picking up the bags and setting them on the bed. She followed him out and sat down. As she pulled the clothes out of the bags, she smiled with each new piece. "You have good taste in clothes, expensive taste. It wasn't necessary for you to spend this kind of money on me. When this is over, I will pay you for everything, your services included. I can't imagine that you will do this for me for free."

"It's not necessary for you to pay me. Call it my civic duty to put this monster out of his misery. I have a few friends who owe me favors, so don't worry about it. I'm just not sure how long it's going to take, and I am sure you want to get back to your life and your family."

"My family is in just as much danger as I am. I cannot let them know anything until it is truly over. Ted was in on this abduction of me. He was there with Sully. He watched as that man whipped me and raped me. This goes deep, deeper than I thought it did. We are talking about some serious corruption here. I have a few friends in the FBI that I can trust. I can be some help. I am good at my job and have some training."

Tate looked at her, before he realized he was standing next to her. His hand came up, and he gently moved her hair, placing it behind her ear. "No offense, beautiful, but your training didn't help you when he got a hold of you the first time."

She stared up into his eyes. "Why are you doing this? Why are you being so kind to me?"

He stood there looking at her. Something deep inside of him was pulling him to her. He needed to cut it off; he wouldn't be able to think straight if he allowed himself to believe he could connect with her. He stepped back, turning to walk away. "At first, I was just doing what any normal human being would do. I was helping someone who needed help. But then I saw your back and it became personal to me. There is only one man who could have done that to you, and I thought I killed him fifteen years ago. Sully, as he calls himself now, is really Frank James. He was my step-father, and he killed my mother with his whip."

Closing his eyes as he heard her gasp behind him. Frozen in his own fears, he just stood there. He didn't hear her move, and he certainly did not expect her to touch him, but she did. She put her hand on his back as she moved around him, wrapping her arms around his waist and hugging him. "I am so sorry for your loss," she whispered into his chest. After a few moments, he gently embraced her.

"Thank you, but it was a long time ago." He moved away from her. "We have a great deal to talk about. We need to get you healed and figure out how to end this fucker and his operation. My guy, Devlin, is in New York watching the man who was supposed to buy you. He is due to check in soon."

"Is that where he was taking me? Sully sold me?" She was confused. "I thought he was taking me out in the woods to kill me."

"No, he sold you." Tate looked at her.

"Do you mind if I change? I think I would feel better if I had some panties and a bra on."

"I don't mind at all, but I don't think you are going to be able to put anything on your back. I had the ladies at the store pick out some kind of tops." He got up and went to the bags. Finding what he was looking for, he pulled them out. "Tops like this, they assured me that women wear these all the time without a bra."

She smiled at him. "You think of everything, don't you?"

"If I'm anything, I am thorough." He smiled and watched her pick out some clothes and disappear into the bathroom.

Tate went to the table and opened the files, spreading the contents on the table and floor. He had a pad of paper and a pen. Teresa still hadn't come out of the bathroom, so he walked up to the door. Again, he heard her sobbing. He knocked softly and said her name. She didn't answer, so he opened the door. She was sitting on the floor in front of the huge two-person tub with her knees pulled up to her chest. He hated to see a woman cry, to see them weak. Women should be empowered, not beaten down.

He didn't plan on it, but he found himself sitting in front of her. She moved to bring herself into the folds of his huge arms. He wrapped his legs around her, cocooning her in his massive frame. His hand moved her hair off her face, and whispered, "It's going to get better. You are safe here."

"He destroyed me. He destroyed my body. Who would want me? Why would anyone want to buy this body?"

"He left you with your life, beautiful. He didn't take that from you, which was his mistake. We will end this. You will find someone who will look past the scars, who will see the incredible woman that you are," he said to her.

"How do you know I'm an incredible woman?"

"You are the youngest Investigative Assistant DA in this city. You have to be pretty incredible to have accomplished such a task. You have superior FBI training, and you graduated top of your class from Harvard."

He felt her chuckle. "And here I sit crying like a child, in the embrace of a complete stranger I have no other choice than to trust."

He laughed. "Yeah, that is pretty pathetic."

She smacked him on the arm and pulled back to wipe her tears. "Thank you." She looked up into his eyes.

He smiled at her, but she could see that it was not real. "It's what I'm here for. You all right now?" She nodded, and he began to unfold his body. Standing he reached for her hand to pull her up. Then he left the bathroom while she changed.

When he walked out, Kelly was standing in the middle of the room with a tray of food. "Be careful, Tate," she reminded him with love in her voice.

"I'm all right. You will be the first to know if I feel myself slipping." He smiled at her.

She nodded. "I made some sandwiches and brownies."

Tate smiled at her. Kelly set the tray on the bed and left. Teresa came out and they ate. When he finished, he got up and went to the table. "I think it's time we started going through all of this. I need you to explain to me what some of it is and where you got your information. If this is a cover-up in our government, then we need to find out who tipped him off and which information is true. Someone could have been feeding you false information."

"Obviously, there is something in here that actually threatened his freedom; otherwise, he wouldn't have taken me."

Together, they sat at the table. Five hours later, Tate looked at her. "You must be tired. Why don't you get some rest, and I'll go fill the guys in and have them get to work on what we know now. See if they can verify some of this."

She nodded and got up. "Tate?" He looked up at her. "I just want to say thank you. It was out of line for me to ask you to hold me. It's just... well, it has been a very long time since someone was tender when they touched me. A very long time since someone..."

Tate stood and lifted her face to meet his. "Anytime."

She smiled at him and walked over to climb on the bed. Tate picked up all the papers and left her to sleep.

CHAPTER FIVE

Tate went down to the study to talk with the guys. "Has Dev checked in?"

"Yeah, he followed this guy to a club called Master's. As far as he can tell, it's just a club. It's by invitation only, and if you get an invitation, you don't turn it down. You become a member. Apparently, your bank account gets you the invitation."

"What kind of bank account?" Tate asked.

"Millions, and you have to be reputable. So, we have no way of getting inside. We can only assume what kind of club it is. Men and women are members."

"Well, we haven't come across anything about this place in anything that Teresa has uncovered. She had no idea she was being sold. She thought she was on her way to being murdered."

"She's talking?" Manny asked.

"Not so much, but I am sure in time she will. What I have here are the files you guys got me. There are some leads in here that I think might be legit. I'm thinking about contacting Williams to see if he can cross over the line and do some digging. Teresa seems to think this goes beyond just the city government. Have Dev find a good place to set up and shoot some of the patrons of this club. Maybe we can get some IDs on them and use that angle."

"You got it. Hey, how are you doing?" Manny asked.

"I'm fine. Let's get busy. I'll contact Williams and see if we can get any outside help."

He left and went to the kitchen. "Hey, Doc, how is she doing?"

"She is healing nicely. The girl was torn up pretty good. She'll be lucky to be able to have children. But, all in all, she is getting better."

"When do you think she will be able to travel?"

Kelly looked at her brother. "What are you thinking, Tate? Are we not safe here?"

"No, we're good. No matter what, Kelly, the safe room is bomb proof so you will be safe here. Teresa has a few contacts in the FBI, guys she trained with that she trusts. I don't trust the phones, so I thought it might be a good idea to go see if they can help us. This is far more complicated and goes a lot deeper than a dirty cop."

"Tate, please, be careful." She stood and put her hand over her heart. "I'm worried about this. I know you, and I know you might feel you can connect with her. Please, just be careful. She is damaged far worse than we are."

He put his hand over hers. "Don't worry, little sister. This..." he tapped his hand, "is safe."

She pushed up on her toes and kissed his cheek. "I know better, big brother," she whispered and smiled at him.

Tate laughed hard and loud as he hugged his sister. "I suppose you do," he whispered in her ear. Letting her go, he looked at Doc. "So, when do you think she can travel?"

"Well, I stopped the antibiotics this morning. She is healing very nicely and quickly. Her appetite is good. I suppose, it's all about how she feels. You've seen her walk around. How is her gait?"

Tate looked at Kelly. "You see her move more than I do."

"She seems fine," Kelly said.

"Physically, I feel great," Teresa said from the doorway. Everyone turned to look at her. "I'm still a bit sore, and it is somewhat uncomfortable to sit for long periods of time. But I am better."

Tate smiled at her. "Good, you think you might be up to a trip to go talk to your buddy at the FBI?"

"Three buddies, and yes, I am. I want this fucker gone, and I want to see Ted's face when I put the cuffs on him and send him to prison with all the guys he's arrested over the years."

Tate nodded. "Then let's do this." Turning, he looked at Kelly. "I am taking everyone but Manny with me. I trust him with my life, so I am trusting him with yours. We should be back in a day or two. You know where the safe room is. Do not leave this house, Kelly, and do not call James. This is it. Once we walk out of here, he will know we are coming. Promise me you will stay put."

"I will promise if you promise to come back alive."

He reached for her and pulled her to his chest. "I promise." He hugged her and then went to fill the guys in.

Back up in his room, he was changing in the closet when Teresa came in. "I'm sorry," she said.

Tate turned to look at her as she was turning around to leave. He smiled and pulled his jeans on. Grabbing his t-shirt and socks, he walked out of the closet. Teresa was sitting on the bed. He watched her look him up and down. He chuckled to himself. "It's all yours," he said, nodding to the closet.

She got off the bed and went to grab some jeans, then went to the bathroom. "I'm going to need a hat and sunglasses. My hair is a dead giveaway, and these bruises can't be hidden with makeup."

"Not a problem. Where do we start?"

"Well, two of my friends are here in Chicago, but I want to start in Washington. But how are we going to get out of the city without being seen?" She walked out of the bathroom as she was putting her hair up in a bun.

Tate chuckled. "Oh, ye of little faith." He handed her a cap and sunglasses. "Do you know how to shoot a gun?"

She raised her eyebrows at him. "FBI training." She pointed to herself.

Tate nodded, bent to pull a gun out of his bag, and handed it to her. "You ready?" he asked.

"As I'll ever be."

She went to walk away, and he reached out, touching her arm. "When we leave here, you listen to me. Every single word, order, or suggestion I give you, you listen to me. If you get yourself killed, we won't have a leg to stand on and he wins."

She nodded. "You don't have to tell me twice. To be honest, I am scared shitless."

He stepped forward and wrapped his arms around her. "Don't worry, I've got you."

She leaned into him and took a deep breath. "Let's go."

They made their way downstairs and to the study. "Guys, this is Teresa. Teresa, this is Manny; he is staying behind. This is Cal, Alex, John, Pete, Joey, and you know Doc." She looked around at the six men, thinking, *Damn this is a testosterone party.*

"Nice to meet you," she said, shaking all their hands.

"Everyone ready?" Tate asked.

"We are up and ready to go in ten," Cal said.

"Good, let's get out there and get back in one piece. Destination DC. Who do we have on ground there?"

"Freemon, Dolby, Fry, and Deckler will be waiting for us when we land," Cal said.

"Let's go then." Tate turned around to leave, and Kelly was standing in the doorway.

"Please, come back to me, big brother," she said to Tate.

Teresa watched the interaction between them. Tate reached up and ran his finger down her cheek. "Stay safe, Kel. I don't know what would become of me if anything happened to you. Use the safe room if you have to." She nodded to him. Teresa noticed she had tears running down her cheeks. Tate turned to Manny. "With your life."

Manny nodded. "Always."

He hugged Kelly, and they left the study. The seven of them made their way to the basement. They walked all the way through to the opposite end of the house. Tate pressed on the wall, and it clicked in and slid away. He walked in and waited for everyone to get through, then he pushed it back. Teresa looked at him and raised her eyebrows.

"Impressive," she said, smiling at him.

Tate laughed. "You ain't seen nothing yet. Come on, we've got a hike before we get to our destination."

"Don't tell me we're going via underground tunnel to DC?" Teresa was being a smart ass.

Cal busted out laughing as they trekked through the passageway. Fifteen minutes later, they came to a ladder. Tate went up first. Teresa couldn't see what he was doing, but she heard something that sounded like a steel door. Then she could see light coming from above her. Cal put out his hand, signaling for her to go. As she climbed, she could feel her heart racing in her chest. When she reached the top, Tate pulled her through the opening. They were in a hanger of sorts; it was covered in camouflage netting. As she looked around, she saw a helicopter and two Jeeps. When she looked at Tate, he smiled and raised his eyebrows at her.

"Climb on in. You can sit in the front if you want."

Shaking her head, she asked, "Which side?"

He put his hand on her elbow, led her to the side she was supposed to sit in, and helped her up. Tossing his bag in the back, he went around and got in. Cal opened the roof, and the guys climbed in. Tate did his check-through and started it up. He pointed to the head-phones, wanting Teresa to put them on.

"You okay?" he asked.

She nodded. He was glad to see the smile on her face. They took off, and Tate hovered, making sure the roof closed, and then they were off. He flew for about thirty minutes, then landed at an airstrip outside of Rockford. Once down, they all climbed out, Cal helping Teresa out. They then made their way to a private jet sitting on the runway.

As they got settled in their seats, Teresa said to Cal, "This is like something out of a James Bond movie."

Cal laughed. "Yeah, we do this shit all the time."

She shook her head and tried to get comfortable. Tate and Joey went to the cockpit, and ten minutes later, they were racing down a runway. Once they were in the air, Tate came to talk to her.

"All right, we need to go over the plan and where we are going to meet this friend of yours. I think it's best if he doesn't know we are there. I am going to have Pete shadow you. I'll be as close to you as I can without being seen. It is best this guy has no clue we are with you. I don't want to tip our hand. Pete is our go-to guy. No one ever sees him or suspects him." He looked at Pete, who was making faces at her.

"Okay, I think the best place to approach him would be outside the train station when he gets home from work. He lives outside the city so it might be best."

"Did Hardt know about your connection to this guy?" Tate asked.

"No, we never discussed my life before him. He knew about my family, and that I went to Harvard, but he didn't know anything else."

"He didn't know about the FBI training?"

"No, I never put that on my resume. No one knew."

Tate nodded. "All right, when we touch down, we'll go to base camp and get you wired, and then we'll get into position."

Teresa nodded, and Tate went back to the cockpit. Joey was looking at him. "Say it," Tate said to him.

"Can you trust this girl? I mean, you rescued her, but did you really rescue her? Kelly keeps warning you about getting too close. Women have this sense about them."

Tate chuckled. "I don't think any woman would endure a whipping just to set me up, do you?"

"Tate, man, I don't mean any disrespect, but we have seen shit worse than that. If this guy is who you think he is, you should be a bit more cautious."

"What makes you think I'm not?"

"Well, for one, we have no plan. We are flying by the seat of our pants. In all the years we've been doing this, we have always had a plan in play before we did recon. I've got a bad feeling about this chick. So do the guys."

Tate sat there looking at him. He didn't feel anything but compassion for her. Maybe Kelly was right; maybe he was too close to this. Frank would know how to get to him, how to make him see red.

"Then there is Josh. Man, how long have we been together as a crew? When have you ever known Josh to let his guard down? Something wasn't right with all that shit. No way should he be dead. Why wasn't it on the news?"

Tate sat there for a few minutes thinking. "You're right. Turn us around. We need a plan, and I need to have a serious chat with our guest."

"It's the right thing to do," Joey said.

"Yeah, I'll be right back. Get a call in to Manny. Have him get Kelly and Taylor out of there. Have him get them to the safe house," Tate said.

"On it, boss."

Tate got up and went to sit with Teresa. "Listen, we need to go back. We're having a problem with the plane, so keep your seat belt on and stay calm." He watched her face. She seemed genuinely concerned, but then, why wouldn't she? Tate touched her arm. "It'll be fine, I'm sure."

She smiled at him, and he went back to the cockpit. Joey looked at him. "There is no answer at the house."

"Fuck," Tate said. His heart was slamming in his chest. He reached into his bag and pulled out his SAT phone. "Kel?"

"Oh my God, Tate, we are in the safe room. Manny didn't make it in. Right after you guys took off in the chopper, all the alarms went off. I was with Taylor, and we made it in, but Manny never came. I'm looking at the monitors. The place is crawling with men. I have no idea what the fuck is happening."

"Listen to me, stay put. No one can get in that room. We are on our way back. Hang in there. You have guns and food in there. They will never get in. Stay put. I will come and get you when it's safe. I'm sorry, Kel. I should have listened to you."

"This is not your fault. I was played as well."

"I love you," Tate said.

"I love you, too. Now, get your ass back here and kick some butt on your way."

He chuckled. "I will. See you soon, Kel." He hung up and looked at Joey. "Manny's out. This shit just got real. I don't want to hurt that bitch, but if something happens to Kelly and Tay, I won't be able to stop myself."

"She's in the safe room. She'll be fine. We should be landing soon."

Ten minutes later, they were on the ground and in the helicopter. Twenty minutes after that, they were on their way through the tunnel. About halfway through, Tate stopped and opened a door. He pushed Teresa in, and the guys followed. He grabbed her by the arm and dragged her into another room. Shutting the door behind him, he told her, "Strip."

"What? Are you crazy?" she yelled.

"Either you take them off or I will. Everything." He turned and grabbed a t-shirt out of his bag and threw it at her. "All of it, now!" He raised his voice.

She stood there defiant, not moving. He took a step toward her. "I said now."

"No!" she shouted.

Tate was on her in an instant. She fought but didn't win. By the time he was done, she was standing there naked. He couldn't help but look at her. He had to admit to himself that she was fucking beautiful, even with the bruises and whip marks. He picked up her clothes, put them in the trash can, and started them on fire. Teresa just watched him. He looked into her eyes, but fear was the only thing he saw.

Tate watched as the clothes burned. When they were finished, he dumped the ashes out on the floor. There was nothing in them. His eyes looked up at her. She was still naked. Reaching in his bag, he pulled out a scanner. Grabbing her arm, he started to scan her. Up the right side and down the left. Across her back, her ass, down the right thigh, then up the left. He grabbed her right foot and then the left. He stood up and ran the scanner across her neck and down her chest, to her stomach and across her pubic bone. The light lit up.

Tate towered over her. "You got something you want to say?" She didn't move, just continued to stare at him. Tate turned and walked to the door. Opening it, he yelled, "Doc get in here."

Doc came in, looking at Teresa. "What's going on?"

Tate shut the door and walked over to her, waving the wand by her crotch. "This is what's going on. We need to find it and get it out."

Doc just stood there looking at her. He nodded to Tate. "Get on the fucking table," Tate said to her, but she didn't move. "I will not tell you again. Get on the fucking table." Teresa didn't move. Tate picked her up and laid her on the table. She didn't fight him, just stared at the ceiling.

Doc went to work trying to locate the tracker. "It's not external. It's internal," he said, looking perplexed. "How the fuck? Better yet, why the fuck would someone do this to another human being?"

"Can you get it out?" Tate was pissed.

"Yes," he said questionably. "Tate, can I talk to you?" Doc got up and left the room. Tate followed him.

"Listen, everything this woman went through was real. She didn't fake the trauma that was inflicted on her. She was brutalized, both sexually and physically. To do this would only traumatize her more."

"Right now, Doc, I really don't give a fuck how she feels. My sister and my niece are upstairs locked in a room. Either you get it out of her or I will."

"I know what is at stake here, but keep in mind, we are talking about her mental state."

Tate was pissed. "I don't give a fucking shit about her mental state. The only two people I love are locked in a room upstairs because of her. My men are being dropped like flies. Get it out of her now, Doc, or I will."

Doc nodded, and they went back into the room. Teresa was still lying on the table. Doc grabbed a chair and sat down between her legs. "I'm sorry about this. It's going to be a bit uncomfortable. Do you want me to tell you what I am doing?"

"Just fucking do it," she hissed.

Tate moved to hold her legs so she didn't kick Doc in the face. It took five minutes for him to get it out. Tate tried not to look at her.

63

He did, however, notice that she was a true redhead. He felt his heart soften a little. She didn't flinch as Doc felt around inside of her, or when he carefully sliced her open to get it out. Tate found himself not wanting Doc to touch her in such an intimate way. But he quickly shook that feeling. She had betrayed them all, and Kelly along with Taylor were trapped upstairs. When Doc finished, Tate let go of her legs.

"Now, get the fuck out of here and leave me alone," she said.

Tate looked at her lying there as she slowly closed her legs. She had tears streaming down her face. They both left. Teresa cried. What she was sent here to do had failed, and now, her family was going to pay the price. Her mother, father, and her sisters, along with her brother and their families were all going to die. She rolled over on the table, bringing her legs up to her chest, and cried.

CHAPTER SIX

Tate watched the monitors. "What's going on?"

"It looks like they wired the house," Cal said.

"What do you mean, wired the house?"

"For sound and video."

"Take an earpiece and go take out the cameras. Are any of those bastards here?" Tate asked.

"As far as I can tell, they all left. Where they got to I don't know."

"Any cameras near Kelly?"

"No, man, they all seem to be in hallways and in your bedroom, the kitchen, and the study," Cal pointed out.

"Kelly is just one floor above us. I'm going to get her. You guide me and let me know if anyone is coming," Tate said, reaching for an earpiece.

"I'll go with you," Pete offered.

"No, you all stay here. I might need you as back-up." Tate walked out the door and headed toward the basement. Pulling his gun out, he made sure the safety was off then opened the door into the basement.

"No cameras yet," he heard in his ear. He kept moving across the basement like a mouse. He headed up the stairs. "Still no cameras," Joey said in his ear. Tate opened the basement door. "Stop. Camera in the hall. I'm sending up Cal. If he sees you, it's over. We can't risk Kelly. Man, just leave her there she is safe in that room. There is enough food for a month. This is stupid, Tate. You are not this careless. She knows what to do."

"Fuck," Tate whispered. He headed back down the stairs and across the basement. He stood by the door to the passageway and listened. He needed to make sure no one was there. No cameras could mean they were waiting. He opened the door and shut it, running a steel beam across it to seal them inside. He didn't walk down the hall; he ran.

Barreling into the room, he looked at Doc. "This shit just got real. I am going in there, and no matter what you hear, do not open that door."

"Tate, don't do this," Doc said.

"Fuck that, Kelly and Taylor are prisoners up there. This ends now. I don't fucking care, Doc. They are all I have left."

He walked into the room where Teresa was still lying on the table naked. When he slammed the door, she jumped but didn't get up. She didn't even open her eyes. Tate moved fast and grabbed her by the throat, lifting her off the table and slamming her against the wall.

"Tell me what the fuck you did and why, and don't leave anything out. If you think for one minute that you can handle what I am prepared to dish out to you, then you are fucking mistaken. What Sully did to you was a fucking piece of cake compared to what I am going to do."

"Fucking do it then. I've got nothing left to lose. By doing what you did to me, you murdered my whole family."

"Well, I guess they'll be glad to see you then." He threw her across the room. She hit the wall like a rag doll and landed hard. He walked out and slammed the door. Walking over to the cabinet, he took out a bottle of Jack and poured himself a tumbler, swallowing it in one drink. He proceeded to pour another. Cal stepped forward, and Tate said one word. "Don't." Cal stopped.

Tate was a huge man at six-feet-four-inches, weighing a sturdy two-hundred and seventy pounds, all of it solid muscle. He scared the shit out of most people. "Doc, you should go make sure I didn't kill her," he said as he downed another drink.

"We've got movement," Joey yelled. Tate turned around to look at the monitors. "I managed to hack into their feed, so I've got audio, too."

It was suddenly very quiet. Doc made his way into the room where Teresa lay like a crumpled piece of paper on the floor. He felt her pulse, shaking his head. "Oh, sweetheart, what have you done?" he said as he counted the beats. He lifted her and laid her on the table, then grabbed a jacket that was in the locker on the wall and covered her with it. "You are going to hurt when you wake up, doll." He moved the hair off her face and saw that Tate had broken her nose. He put his hands on either side of her nose and jerked it back into place. There was nothing more he could do until she woke up and told him what hurt. So, he made his way back into the other room. Tate looked at him. "She's alive."

Tate shook his head. "I need to get to Kelly and Taylor."

Watching the monitors, they counted ten men in all moving through the house. None of them even came close to Kelly and Taylor, so they were clueless to the panic room. "We need to get in there and take care of these fuckers." The guys agreed.

"Tate, listen to me. They are safest in that room. We need to end Sully and then get them out. She would only be a target, and you would spend more time worrying about them, which could result in you making a mistake," Cal said, trying to reason with him.

"I know you're right, but emotion seems to be overriding my logic. I need to think." He picked up the walkie talkie and left. He started toward the other end of the tunnel, away from the exit into the house. Talking into the walkie talkie, he said, "Hey, Kel, you there?"

"Yeah, hold on, Taylor is sleeping," she whispered. "Okay, what's up?"

"Sully is Frank, and he knows if he gets you, I will do anything he wants."

"I figured as much. How did he find us, Tate? How did he know it was us? We changed our names."

"I don't know. But, Kel, you have to stay in there." He waited for her to blow up at him.

"I know," she whispered.

"Can you do this? You guys will be good for a month; can you stay in there until I come to get you?" He leaned against the wall.

"My main concern is Taylor. Tate, if he got his hands on her…"

Tate closed his eyes, and tears spilled down his cheeks. He remembered what Frank had done to her. How he raped her and whipped her. He knew Frank would do the same to Taylor. "I know. So, you'll stay put?" He tried to be tough, but Kelly knew him. She knew all about how scared he was.

"I will. Tate, what about Teresa?"

"Sully implanted her with a tracking device. He put it inside her fucking pussy. Doc got it out, and then I nearly killed her. She said something to me, something that is bothering me. She told me that she didn't care what I did to her, that by doing what I did, I murdered her entire family. I think Sully threatened her to do this. I kind of lost it, and I hurt her."

"Oh, Tate, she is a pawn in this. She didn't fake what happened to her. He did those things to her. He kidnapped her. He probably made her believe she was doing the right thing. You need to help her. Tate, how are you?"

"I just keep seeing her face, Kel. I can't get her face out of my head. She ripped my heart out."

"I know. Her death was not your fault. You didn't kill her."

"No, but I didn't do anything to stop it, either, so I am just as guilty as that guy who raped her and slit her throat."

"Hey, she was playing the mind game with you. She was the one who called you to rub your face in it."

"When I look at my hands, sometimes, I can still see her blood."

"I know, but Tate, you don't love Teresa like you loved Jenny. You were all in with her. Teresa is a victim as well, only she survived. How many girls has he taken? How many girls have not survived his punishment? Our own mother didn't. Do this for mom, Tate. Do this for all those girls out there who don't have a choice. Do it for

Taylor so she can be safe. Do it for you so you can finally let go of Jenny."

"I love you, Kelly," he whispered.

"I love you, too, Tate. Go be our hero. Save us. You have thirty days," Kelly whispered.

"Don't leave that room. Promise me, Kelly, that you will stay there."

"I promise, Tate. Now go." She turned off the walkie talkie.

Tate put his head down and let the tears flow. The last time he cried was that night in the alley while he held Jenny in his arms knowing she was dead, her blood soaking him. He heard footsteps and looked up as Doc was kneeling beside him.

"She is alive and awake. She is talking or wants to talk to you."

"Did I hurt her?" Tate said.

"Broke her nose, but I fixed that. You all right?" Doc asked.

"Never better. Kelly is staying put until we finish this. It's the only place I know she is safe. So, let's go do this." He stood, and they went back to the room where Teresa sat dressed in the t-shirt he'd thrown at her before he stripped her.

"What the fuck could you possibly say to me that would stop me from breaking your fucking neck?" he shouted at her.

He had to admit to himself that she was one stubborn woman. She squared her shoulders and did not cower away from his loud voice and ominous presence.

"He knew he wasn't going to break me. Jesus, he had me in that fucking dungeon for six fucking months. I had heard conversations he had with Ted and some other guys I didn't know but could point out. He was looking for you. He has been looking for you for fifteen years, according to Sully. Apparently, he found you. He finally made me an offer I couldn't refuse. He put my family on the table. Either I do what he said and give my life to you, because he knew you would kill me once you figured it out, or Sully would kill my entire family. He is a very convincing man. After he let six men beat me and rape me, I agreed. Ted was the one who implanted the tracker in me. He said you weren't the fucking kind so there would be no way you would find it.

"The guy in the car was supposed to drop me off at your cabin, and

I was supposed to stumble along your path so you could find me and then help me. He knows things about you. He knows all your men. He is going to take you one at a time."

Tate laughed, "He may think he knows me, but he doesn't have a fucking clue."

"He told me that you would contact Kelly and she would come to help take care of me. He knows you have a soft spot for abused women. He wants Kelly and Taylor; he knows you would come for them and keep them close to you where you thought they'd be safest. I was to lead you away with some sort of story so he could get to Kelly. He didn't get her, did he?"

"Trust me, if he had, you wouldn't be talking to me right now," Tate snapped at her.

"When I saw your back that day in the bathroom, I knew you were his victim also. I don't know the history you have with him; I don't want to know. But that man will move heaven and earth to end you."

Tate looked at her. "I don't trust a word out of your fucking mouth. I am going to lock you in this room with food and water. I don't care if you fucking die in here. You put the only two people I love in grave danger. You led that son of a bitch to my door step."

She jumped off the table and got in his face. "Are you fucking serious? He didn't need me to get to you. He knows everything there is to know about you. Fuck you, Tate Miles, and the fucking horse you rode in on. That mother fucker knows how much money you have in the bank, right down to the penny. He knows everything. Leave me here, go ahead. I don't give a shit. But don't you dare think for one minute that you scare me. You know why? Because for six months I have fucking danced with the devil himself inside the walls of hell. So, fuck you!"

Never had he met someone brave enough to go toe to toe with him. No wonder she was an Investigative ADA. He felt proud to know her. But he wasn't about to let her know that. He stared her down and then turned and walked out of the room, locking the door behind him. Walking up to the bottle of Jack, he poured a glass and drank it down. He picked up the bottle and looked at it, throwing it against the wall. "Fuck," he said.

The guys just stood there looking at him. "I am so fucking done playing this game. Let's go blow this son of a bitch out of the water. I don't give a flying fuck how far or how deep this goes. I am done. If any of you want to back down, then do it now. You may end up dead. The choice is yours, and I will not hold anything against any of you."

None of them moved. It was Cal who spoke. "I don't know how many times you have saved my life or stuck your neck out for me, both in life and on the battlefield. I'm with you, man."

None of them backed down.

"Thanks. Now, find a way to gather everyone here. I think if we cut the head off this fucking snake, the cards will fall where they should. First, we are going to clean house." He tilted his head up. "Vests on, everyone. If this bastard wants to play, let's give him our best game. Hold nothing back, guys. Joey, you stay here and watch the cameras. Earpieces, everyone. We are going in SEAL style."

One by one, they walked across the passageway to another room that was completely hidden. They donned vests, earpieces, the total gear. They were loaded up with clips, guns, knives, grenades, and flash grenades. When they were finished, they walked down to the ladder and, one by one, climbed out. They worked their way back to the house, taking men down as they went.

There was no talking among them. Joey was in their ears telling them what was coming. The six men moved silently. There were more than ten men; they took out eight outside. Once in the house, Joey led them through. When it was over, Tate walked up to one of the cameras, pulled it out of its spot, and said right into it, "I'm coming for you, Frank. There is no hiding from me this time." He dropped the camera and stepped on it.

Turning, he moved back through the house as they emptied it and headed back into the woods. Once back in the tunnel, they made their way to the ammo room, taking off their gear.

Back in the room with Joey, Tate began, "We need to get everyone here. All in all, we are thirty strong. Sully may know who we are, but I can assure you he has no clue how we run. Time to end this. We have thirty days until Kelly runs out of food. For now, we do nothing but wait for everyone to get here. Joey, get on it. I'm going to get some rest. I suggest you all do the same."

"What about Teresa?" Doc asked.

"Get her some food. Other than that, I don't give a shit. She set me up, and she nearly got Kelly and Taylor killed. This bastard is a sick fuck, and as far as I'm concerned, the sooner we end this, the sooner I can get that bitch out of my life." Tate walked out of the room, slamming the door behind him. He made his way to another room filled with cots and crashed.

Tate's sleep was filled with nightmares. Filled with the horrors of his childhood. His sleep wasn't sleep at all, but a doorway to his past, a past that molded him into the man he was. A past that drove a teenage boy to murder. A past he would like to forget. Finally giving up, he got up and went to check on Teresa. He half-expected her to jump him when she heard the key in the lock, but when he opened the door and saw her sitting in the corner just staring at him, he felt bad. He couldn't imagine how she felt. How many times had she been locked in a dark room, alone and scared. She wasn't shaking; she was just very still. Tate went in and shut the door behind him. Walking over, he sat down on the floor in front of her.

"I am not going to apologize for what happened today. You put my sister and my niece in grave danger," he said as nicely as he could.

Her eyes moved from his chest to his mouth and then seared into his eyes. "My whole family is going to be murdered now. There is no way to stop him," she whispered. Tate watched as a tear fell from her eye.

He reached up and wiped it from her cheek. "No, they're not. I already got them out. They are safe. They have no idea what is happening. I told my men not to say a word to them, but they are all safe. Mother, father, sisters, brother, nieces, nephews, dogs, cats, and if I am not mistaken, a few fish and a bird."

Tate could see the relief wash over her. "How did you know?"

"I am a man of many means. I told you in the beginning, you were safe with me. You should have come clean with me."

"I know it's no excuse, but the thought of him letting me go was something I needed. The things he did to me, the things he let others do to me. I still can't believe I am alive. He gave me an out so I took it. I didn't know you. I didn't care about you or what he planned for you. I cared about myself. He knows everything there is to know about you."

Tate chuckled. "No, beautiful, he doesn't have a clue. He only knows what the public knows, what the government knows. He doesn't know shit. I will end him, and together, we will free those women, or at least stop him from hurting anyone else. That fucker killed my mother. I will end him."

"I want to help you. My contacts I told you about are real. My role in Sully's plan was to get you away from the house. He wants Kelly and her daughter. He said that he could kill you if he had them. That you would come for them. He is a sick fucker, and I am more than willing to help you. I don't know much about where we were, but I believe we were in the basement of the Black Cat. It's where he takes all his girls."

"Tell me about your time there, not as his prisoner but as one of his girls."

"It wasn't easy getting a job there." She chuckled. "I was considered fat. The woman who interviewed me told me I had to lose fifteen pounds, and when I did, to come back. The woman actually felt me up. She said that the boss didn't like fake tits." She shook her head. "So, I lost fifteen pounds and went back. I was hired. I danced mostly. I'm sure that is something I can put on my new resumé. I mostly listened when I could, played dumb, and gathered my information. Sully usually breaks his girls in. Sleeps with each and every one of them."

"But not you?" Tate asked.

She shook her head. "While I was there, the girls would just disappear. One night, they would be working, and the next night, they would be gone. It would happen all the time, but Sully worked his way down the line. There were a few girls who were hired before me that hadn't been broken in. But I spoke to many of the girls that were. He did awful things to them. Having experienced his brand of being broken in, I know now what they meant. I figured out what he was doing. He would beat them into submission. Some were fast. Some he kept for himself, but most of them went quickly. I followed them a few times when that guy who had me would take one of the girls."

"Where did they go?"

"He would take them out to the lake, and they were put on a boat. From there, it's anyone's guess. I didn't have a boat to follow."

"Do you know where at the lake?"

She nodded. "So, I gathered enough intel with pictures, and a few of his regular girls said they would testify. He had them all so scared. But I was taking all the evidence I had gathered over the time I was there, and I was on my way to the Grand Jury hearing, and now, I am here with you."

"What role does Ted have in all of this?" Tate asked.

Teresa shook her head. "He was never my boyfriend. He just used me. From listening, after Sully had me, Ted's role was to find him young girls who had gotten themselves in trouble and bring them to Sully. Apparently, he would find runaways, or girls who were in juvy, and give them the speech about having someone look out for them, then he would bring them to Sully. Most of those girls were sold into the sex trade. I know quite a few of them went to a place in New York called Master's."

"I'll be right back," Tate said and left the room, locking the door behind him. He walked down the hall to wake up Cal. "Hey, man, we need to talk."

Cal nodded and got up to follow Tate into the hall. They made their way into the room with all the fire power. Tate turned to Cal. "Listen, I was just talking to Teresa. She said the girls that were sold, were sold to whoever owns that Master's place in New York. We need to find out who owns it. I also want a day to day on the three guys Teresa knows in the FBI. I want to make sure they are safe to have a chat with. If this shit goes as deep as I think it does, we are going to need all the help we can get. Our contacts that are legit are not up for option. Sully thinks he knows our operations, but I know he only knows what the public and the government know. He hasn't a clue about anything else. Gather everyone and have them meet us in three days on the island. I want this over sooner rather than later. Kelly has twenty-nine days left in there, and we need to have this over with by then. Wake the guys if you have to, but I want everything you've got, like yesterday."

"You've got it, but are you sure about this fight, Tate?" Cal asked.

"I know you don't know much about my past, my childhood. But Sully is my stepfather, Frank. I thought I killed that fucker fifteen years ago, but somehow, he survived. The thought that he is stealing and kidnapping young women to sell them into the sex trade is enough for me to get involved. My past connection means nothing. I will end him if it's the very last thing I do on this planet." Tate slapped him on the back. "I'll be with Teresa. She has a great deal to tell me, so knock only when you have something to tell me."

Cal nodded. Tate went back to Teresa, and Cal got busy. Walking into the room, he found her still sitting in the corner. He locked the door and went to sit on the floor in front of her.

"I have Cal working on some things. Tell me about these three friends of yours."

She sat there looking into his eyes. "Why would you do this? Why would you help me, knowing that I was willing to trade your life for mine?" she whispered.

Tate reached up and put her hair behind her ear, gently brushing his thumb along her cheek as he did it. "Let's just say I have a soft spot for damsels in distress."

She smiled. "I am far from a damsel."

He cupped her face in his hand. "I am the man who will never underestimate your ability to stay alive and endure. To me, you are a strong woman who survived spending six months with a monster." He lowered his voice. "My mother didn't stand a chance against him."

She moved slowly. Reaching up with her tiny hand, she gently touched his jaw. "I am so sorry for what he did to her, to you, to Kelly."

Tate just sat there looking at her. She leaned up on her knees and then moved into his lap, wrapping her arms around his neck and pulling herself close to hug him. Tate sat there for a minute, not knowing what to do. Slowly, his hands moved, and he encircled her, pulling her into his hold. She felt warm in his arms, so fragile and tiny. He imagined she had been starved, and probably needed a good twenty or thirty pounds on her tiny frame. But she felt so good in his embrace. He bent his head into her neck and, catching her scent, thought she smelled like heaven. When her chest touched his, he felt the warmth all the way to his toes. He gently pulled her away. Looking into her eyes, he said in almost a whisper, "This wasn't part of the plan, was it? To seduce me, make me crazy?"

She shook her head. "This is me, thanking you and comforting you. I am free of Sully, and my family is safe because of you, and I just needed to feel a bit of comfort. I haven't felt anything in the past six months but brutality. Thank you, Tate. I cannot begin to tell you how sorry I am for my part in this." She turned her eyes down, and her voice got even softer. "I sometimes wish he would have just killed me."

Tate tipped her face up so her eyes met his. They were filled with unshed tears. "Don't say that," he whispered as the first tears spilled over the rims of her eyes and onto her cheeks. With his thumb, he wiped them from her cheeks. "Don't ever say that," he rasped out. He found himself moving closer to her, placing his forehead on hers. "One month and you can go home. One month and you can have your life back. One month and I will be a distant memory." He closed his eyes and took a deep breath.

Teresa tipped her head up. Tate could feel the warmth of her breath on his lips. Then she moved again, and the feather-light touch of her lips against his shook him to his core. He pulled his head back, looking at her. She was crying.

"What's wrong, beautiful?"

Through tears and sobs, she said, "This is the first time in six months I have felt safe."

He chuckled. "This is the first time in two years that I have felt, period." He pulled her into his embrace and held her while she cried. He wasn't sure how long they sat there, when there was a knock on the door. Tate lifted her and sat her on the floor then got up to open the door. Cal was standing there, and he nodded at Tate. Turning, Tate told Teresa, "I'll be back in a little while. Why don't you try to get some sleep?" Teresa nodded at him, and he left, locking the door behind him.

"What's up?" He asked Cal.

"You aren't going to believe this. It took a while to figure it all out. There are dummy corporations, fake people, but in the end, that club, Master's, well, it is owned by two people. Sully and that guy Alex Welsh."

"Yeah I figured Sully's hand was in there somewhere. Thanks, Cal. Have you heard from Dev?"

"Not since yesterday."

Tate nodded. "Keep working on it." He walked out into the hallway and pulled out one of the burner phones, dialing Dev.

"Yeah," Dev answered in a groggy voice.

"Sorry to wake you man, but the shit is about to get real. What do you know?" Tate said into the phone.

"Well, I know that there are a lot of young girls in that place. I've got two guys on film dragging two young girls in the back way. This is a fucking sex house, I'm sure of it."

"Yeah, I think you're right. Listen, I need you to get the fuck out of there. Leave now, just leave everything running. We can monitor it from here. I don't have a good feeling about this. With Josh and Manny out, I need you safe. Get to the island now."

"You've got it. I am already dressed. I'll see you in a few hours." Dev hung up.

"Fuck," Tate whispered to the empty hall. Somewhere deep inside, he knew that this was the last time he would hear his buddy's voice. Shaking his head, he looked at the phone, knowing the call he was about to make was one he'd hoped he never had to make. Dialing, he closed his eyes as he pressed the phone to his ear.

"Yeah," the voice on the other end answered.

"Yeah, it's me. The shit just got real. It's all or nothing."

"Tell me what you need, buddy," the voice answered.

"I need it all, and I need it stealth." Tate squeezed his eyes. He knew that blood would run in the streets of Chicago, but there was no other way, not with Kelly and Taylor at risk.

"Twelve hours," the voice said, and the line went dead.

Tate dropped the phone on the floor and crushed it. He took the walkie talkie out of his pocket. "Kelly, you there?"

"Yeah, what's up?"

"I'm leaving. In the back of the room, behind the vent, is a safe. The combination is your birthday. Right, left, then right, and then left again. Inside is a gun and a phone. Do not use the phone unless you have to. There is one number programed into it. This is going to be the last time you will hear from me until I come and get you."

"Tate?"

"Yeah, baby."

"Are you scared?"

"Of losing you, yes. Kelly, I will make it safe for you. I hope it's me that comes to get you. If it's not, there is five million in a bank in Georgia in your name. Take it and disappear. Twenty-nine days and you run. Don't look back. If I survive this, I will find you."

"I love you, big brother. I know you have to do this, and I know why. But I wish you wouldn't. I am not ready to lose you," she whispered.

"I know, baby. I love you, Kelly. Never forget that."

He heard her sniffing. "I love you, Tate. Please, come back and get us. Please." She was crying now.

"I will do everything I can. I have to go now," he whispered.

Kelly was shaking her head and sobbing as Tate ended the conversation, shutting off his radio. He wiped his eyes and pushed off the wall. Walking back into the room, he said, "Cal, what's it look like out there?"

"Calm."

"We need to load up and get out now. We have a long trip ahead of us. Dev, hopefully, is meeting us there. Let's get moving."

Doc looked at Tate; they all did. He just nodded, and they knew it was go time. Tate unlocked the door, grabbed some clothes out of the locker, and tossed them to Teresa. "Get dressed. We're leaving."

She nodded and started undressing right in front of him. Pete walked in and stood there watching Teresa.

"What?" Tate shocked him. He snapped his head to look at him.

"Ready," Pete said and walked out.

CHAPTER SEVEN

Teresa was dressed and standing just behind Tate. "I'm ready."

Tate turned and put his finger on her chin, tilting her face up so he could look her in the eyes. "If you turn on me, I will break your fucking neck."

Pulling her head out of his grip, she squared her shoulders, facing him. "If you fuck this up, I will break yours. I want this son of a bitch, and I am going to enjoy myself while I slowly torture his ass." She moved past him, pushing into his side as she walked out of the room.

Tate shook his head as a smile creeped across his lips. She was a bad ass, that was for sure. Spinning on his heels, he turned and followed her out of the room.

"Let's go," Tate said to the room.

The guys followed him to the room across the hall and gathered what they would need: vests, guns, knives, grenades, etc. Tate turned to Teresa, who was just outside the door, and handed her a vest. "Put this on. Hopefully, we don't have to worry, but I would hate to have gotten you this far for it to all end once we leave here."

She reached for the vest. "Thanks," she said, taking it from him and strapping it on.

Handing her a gun, Tate said, "I can trust you with this, right?" He tried to hide the smile on his face.

She looked at him and smirked. "I don't know. Can you?" She reached for the gun and belt. Taking it from him, she strapped it on her hips and then took the gun out and checked to make sure it was loaded. Tate stood there watching her, no longer able to hide the smile.

Without realizing it, his hand reached up, and he brushed his knuckles along her cheek. Her eyes looked up at him. "You listen to everything I say. Don't hesitate or you will be dead. He is not fucking around. Frank wants us both dead."

Nodding, Teresa said, "I won't hesitate. Will you?"

Tate wrapped his huge hand around her neck and pulled her flush with him. His mouth was only inches from hers. Teresa swallowed, feeling his breath on her face. "Oh, you will survive this, beautiful."

Cal poked his head in the door, clearing his throat. "You two ready, or are we going to have tea next?' He chuckled.

His eyes never leaving hers, he said, "Yeah, we're ready." He let go of her neck reluctantly and stepped around her, leaving Teresa to gather herself and calm down.

She smiled. That man gave her body a charge. After everything that had happened to her, after shutting down for the six months while Sully tortured her, she believed she would never feel again. But now, now, she felt herself coming alive. Turning, she followed them out into the hall, and they took off on a jog down the tunnel to the hatch.

Once the Jeeps were checked for any kind of tracking devices, they loaded up and took off through the woods. They didn't hit any roads, and about three hours later, they stopped.

Tate got out and looked at Teresa. "We walk from here." She nodded and got out of the Jeep. Standing by as the guys covered the vehicles, she couldn't help but notice the way Tate's muscles rippled along his shoulders with every movement. Hell, all the other guys were built just like him, too. These men were huge and fit. She felt herself smile.

Tate looked at her, "Care to let us in on the joke?"

Chuckling, she said, "I've just never seen so much testosterone in one place. Even with all my training, our F.B.I. guys are nothing compared to all of you."

Cal laughed. "That's because we were all breastfed." That sent the rest of them into a fit of laughter.

Tate smiled at her and said just loud enough for her to hear, "You ain't seen nothing yet." Teresa's body shuddered at the thought of seeing the rest of him.

Once everything was covered, they took off hiking. It was another two hours in the pitch black through the woods before they finally stopped. Joey and Pete took off while the others sat and waited. When they returned, they walked for another twenty minutes to the edge of what looked like a small river. Teresa noticed there were a few Zodiacs in the water. She stood by and watched the guys load into them.

Tate turned to her. "Let's go."

She was frozen in place. "I can't swim."

Climbing out of the boat, Tate walked up to her and said, "Good thing we aren't going swimming."

"No, I can't do this. I can't get in that boat." Panic rose up inside her.

Tate bent and picked her up. "I won't let anything happen to you," he told her as he carried her to the boat.

"No, no, no..." Teresa tried to fight him.

He squeezed her a bit a tighter, whispering in her ear, "Don't worry, beautiful. I've got you." Stepping into the boat, he sat down with her in his arms. Pete gave him a funny look, but Tate ignored him.

They were in the boats for about an hour, traveling slowly down the small river. The entire time, Tate held Teresa close to his chest. When the boats stopped, they climbed out and he set her on the ground.

"See, no swimming." He smirked to her. She half-chuckled.

The guys pulled the Zodiacs out of the water and into the brush then covered them up.

"Let's go," Tate said, and they started hiking again. About twenty minutes later, they emerged onto a beach and made their way to a small marina.

Teresa reached up to touch Tate's arm. "Please, tell me we are not getting on another boat."

Tate chuckled. "I can't do that, but this boat is a bit bigger. You can lay down and rest on this one."

"That's not any more assuring than the last one. I don't think I can do this."

"You can and you will. Now, come on. We need to get out of here before the sun comes up. Pete and Joey should be back in a few." He turned and walked toward Alex, just as Pete and Joey walked up.

"Everything's good to go. The boat is clean," Joey said. "We need to get out of here. The sun is due to come up soon."

Tate looked out over the lake, the sky was getting lighter on the horizon. "Let's go," he said as he reached to grab Teresa's hand. "We need to keep moving. Manny keeps some medicine on the boat because he always gets sick." He chuckled. "I'm sure it will help you sleep. We won't arrive until its dark, so you can sleep below deck." Teresa nodded and followed behind him.

They walked along the shoreline to a small marina, where there were just five boats docked. Two were smaller speed boats, two were big fishing boats, and behind those was a huge cabin cruiser. Teresa looked up at Tate. "What the hell is that?"

He chuckled loudly. "That would be Josh's boat. He would go out on the lake alone on his down time. When you do what we do, and have done what we have done, solitude is something all of us enjoy. It's necessary sometimes to get your shit together."

"And where is it you go?" she asked.

"My cabin," he responded simply, like she should have known.

Nodding her head, she climbed aboard. Everyone moved down off the deck and into the galley. "I'm going to get Teresa set up and get her some of Manny's pills. Pete, get us moving. Remember, no noise, just get us out of here." Pete nodded and Tate grabbed Teresa's hand and led her down into the belly of the boat. There was a small hallway lined with a few doors. Tate led her to the end of the hall and through a door. "You can sleep in here." He moved aside so she could see the space. There was enough room to move around a huge king-sized bed, but that was it. There were a few windows that were covered with drapes, and a small door to her left. Tate reached for the door. "This is a bathroom if you need it." He walked in and opened the cabinet, taking out a pill bottle. "Here, Manny always took two of these, but he was a big guy. You should probably just take one." He handed her the pills. "I need to get up top. I'll check on you in a few hours, once we get out on open water." Moving past her, he opened the door. Teresa reached for his arm.

"Please, don't let me drown," she whispered.

Tate reached out to run the back of his knuckles down her cheek. "Don't worry, beautiful. There is a life jacket in this cabinet right here." He touched the cabinet to his right.

Teresa nodded and opened the pill bottle. Tate smiled and left her to it. She went in the small bathroom and got a drink to swallow the pill. When she came out, she laid on the bed, hoping to find some relief from the panic rising in her chest. As she lay there, she could hear the guys up top talking and getting things moving, so she closed her eyes. She must have fallen asleep, because when the engines roared to life, she bolted upright in the bed. The boat surged forward, and they were moving, and fast. She laid back down, feeling the effects of the pill taking over. As the boat bounced across the water, Teresa's fear welled up. She got up and opened the cabinet and grabbed the life jacket. Hurrying, she put it on and laid back down in the bed, squeezing her eyes shut and clutching to a pillow.

About an hour had passed, and she had fallen asleep again. Tate popped his head in to check on her a few hours later. He opened the door as he let his eyes adjust to the darkness of the room. He could see her tiny body curled in a ball with the pillow clutched to her. His heart swelled as he realized she was wearing the life jacket. Taking a deep breath, he stepped in and gently closed the door. He felt himself being drawn to her, and before he realized it, he was sitting on the bed beside her.

Teresa felt the bed shift as his weight came down on it, and she turned her head.

"You ok?" Tate asked.

"I'm not sure, but whatever is in those pills is knocking me on my ass."

Tate chuckled. "Yeah, Manny was just as frightened of the water as you. It's funny, considering he was a SEAL. I just came to check on you. We have a few more hours before we get to where we need to be."

He went to stand, and her little hand came out and touched his arm. "Don't leave," she whispered.

Tate closed his eyes and swallowed the lump in his throat. "If I stay..." he whispered, not trusting himself to say the right thing. He wanted her. He wanted her bad, but she was the job. He couldn't cross that line. He knew she could destroy him if he let her in.

"I don't want to be alone," she whispered into the darkness.

"Beautiful," he said more to himself than anyone. The internal struggle was beyond him. His body was moving, his brain shutting down, as he climbed back on the bed and laid down next to her. "This is not a good idea." She rolled over to snuggle up next to him. Tate's body came alive; he hadn't felt this way ever. Even with Jenny, he never felt like this. His arms wrapped around her as he turned to face her. They were laying side by side on the bed.

Teresa looked up into his eyes. "Thank you," she whispered, her warm breath caressing his face. He just stared into her eyes, searching for a meaning behind her actions. Could this be a trick to sidetrack him? So many things he needed to be cautious about, but this feeling deep inside of him seemed to be clouding his mind. He could see the honesty in her eyes. Her trust in him was breathtaking. He closed his eyes, trying to regulate his breathing. This woman, the warmth of her body next to him, the feeling of her breath on his neck was all more than he could bear. Slowly, he opened his eyes to see her deep green ones looking right into his soul.

"This is very difficult for me, beautiful," he whispered as his hand came up and gently moved the hair from her face. He swallowed, and with no control over his body, his head moved in a little. Teresa's breath hitched in her chest as he moved closer. "I shouldn't be doing this."

Teresa moved, closing the small space between them. Tate swallowed when he felt her breath on his face.

"God help me," he said into her mouth as their lips gently touched. Her mouth closed around his bottom lip, his around her top lip. He felt her teeth gently bite down on his lip, and he lost his mind, bringing his hand up around the back of her neck and pulling her in. He deepened the kiss. She opened her mouth to him. The kiss was gentle and tender, as he swiped his tongue across hers. The little moans escaping her pushed into his mouth with each breath she took. Tate was losing control, something he never allowed himself to do with a woman. He slowly ended the kiss and pulled back, moving his entire body away from hers. "I'm sorry." He moved off the bed, adjusting his hard cock in his pants. Turning back to Teresa, who was now sitting in the middle of the bed, he said, "That will never happen again. I am sorry." He left the room and closed the door quietly behind him. Taking a deep shaky breath, he whispered, "Fuck," under his breath. *This is the worst fucking idea I have ever had.*

Teresa laid down on the bed, hugging the pillow as the tears slowly slipped from her eyes. *He doesn't want me. I am damaged goods. No one will ever want me. I am going to kill that fucking bastard.* Her mind closed off, and sleep engulfed her.

Tate made his way to another cabin and sat on the edge of the bed with his head in his hands as he tried to make sense of what the hell just happened. She was a client. Even if she didn't hire him, she was a fucking client. She had been raped and tortured within an inch of her life, and here he was kissing her. He shook his head. He would have gone all the way. He knew this; he could feel it deep inside. He wanted her, and he was the kind of man who took what he wanted. Countless women since Jenny he had been with, he had taken and left. This one, though, she was different. She made him feel. Hell. He looked at the door. This one, she is dangerous, definitely dangerous.

While he sat there looking at the door, there was a knock. "Yeah," he said, half expecting Teresa when the door opened.

"Hey, man, Dev is on the phone," Joey said.

Tate furrowed his brow. "Impossible. What phone?"

"I don't know, man. A phone started ringing. I found it in the galley."

Tate cut him off. Standing and moving like lightning past him, he said, "Get the fuck off this boat. Get everyone off now." He ran to the cabin Teresa was in, grabbing her off the bed like a doll, and took off running. He made it to the upper deck and jumped off the side of the boat just as it exploded, knocking him out and sending Teresa flailing through the air and into the dark, cold water.

Teresa came up out of the water, screaming for help. But the only sounds she could hear were her own screams. The glowing flames from the burning boat was all there was in the pitch black, and it was slowly sinking. She was flailing her arms, trying to figure out how to swim, but she had no experience. Fear and terror were the emotions running through her. She couldn't remember ever feeling like that, not even when Sully had her chained to the ceiling. Spitting water out of her mouth, she screamed, "Tate, help me! Anyone! Is anyone out there?" Not realizing she was moving through the water, her arm hit something. She grabbed onto it, not realizing what it was, and panicked. She pulled herself to the object as it rolled in the water in front of her, and came face to face with Joey. After only a moment, she realized that what she was hanging onto was the mangled upper half of his body. That's all there was of him. Screaming, she pushed it away, trying her hardest to get away from him.

Screaming again as she hit something else, terrified to turn around, she closed her eyes to face whatever was touching her in the near darkness. As her eyes opened, she saw Tate's face. "Oh God, Tate." She tried to grab a hold of him, his body starting to sink into the water. "No, no," she sobbed. "Come on, please, Tate. Please, wake up." She cried as she patted his face. Remembering her CPR training, she felt for a pulse. Her hands were shaking so badly she couldn't feel anything. Reaching up, she felt his mouth and nose for breath. "Oh

God, come on, wake up," she whispered when she felt the warmth of his breath on her fingers.

The boat was nearly completely submerged, and with it, what little light there was to help her see. Teresa struggled to get her arms under his to hold him up, hoping her life jacket would hold them both above water. Barely able to keep her head above the water, she forced herself to relax and just float. Hopefully, he would wake up.

What seemed like hours went by as the waves lapped against her, the water constantly in her face. The water was so cold, her body shivered uncontrollably, and her arms grew weaker by the minute. She was so tired, but she knew if she let him go, he would drown. Through her own sobs, she begged him to wake up. "Please, Tate. I can't hold on much longer. Please, wake up." Nothing, no response. Time moved by, and she grew weaker and weaker. Eventually, she felt her arms slipping, and she was too exhausted and too weak to fight it much longer. The sky was turning lighter, which meant it was nearly day break.

In the middle of Lake Michigan was the same as being ship wrecked at sea. No one would ever find them. No one knew where they were. She didn't even know where they were going or how close they were to their destination. As her eyes closed for the hundredth time, it was harder and harder to open them. She thought she heard something and forced her heavy lids to open. She didn't think she had the energy to call out. Not that anyone could or would hear her.

She managed to lock her hands across Tate's chest as her eyes closed again. She was tired and had nothing left in her. This time, her eyes didn't open again. Exhausted, freezing, terrified, and in the middle of a lake where no one would ever find her was how her life would end. Giving up was the only option, her body shutting down from being in the water for so long. It was easy to let it go, easier than she had ever imagined. There was no fear where she was going. she was nearly there. In the back of her mind, she felt her hands give way, her arms finally relaxing. The weight of the man she held in her arms slowly slid from her body. Then bliss. She was floating. There was nothing but peace for her. No pain, no cold, no fear. Just peace.

CHAPTER EIGHT

"What the fuck was that?" Parker Stone yelled out as he looked out over the water. A huge fireball lit up the night sky.

"Some kind of explosion, it looks like," Jimmy said as he looked at Stone.

"Fuck," he yelled as he took off running toward the dock with six of his crew close behind him. "Get me the fucking coordinates," he yelled out as he jumped on the boat.

One of the guys untied the boat as Stone started the engines and took off out into the dark waters of Lake Michigan at full throttle. The boat they were on was one he'd got from one of his not so legal friends, down in Columbia, for a security job he did last year. Hitting top speed of nearly seventy, they took off into the darkness.

"What are those coordinates, Jimmy?" Stone yelled above the wind.

Jimmy yelled out the coordinates, and Stone entered them into the navigation system. "Fuck," he said. They were about three hours out; it would be nearly dawn before they reached the spot. "How much extra fuel do we have?"

"We can refill two times," someone yelled out.

Time moved forward as they zipped across the black night. No full moon, so it was even darker than usual. About an hour out, Stone turned to see Max standing next to him. Stone nodded, and Max took over. He made his way into the cabin.

"What the hell is going on, Stone?" Jimmy asked.

"I'm not sure yet, but I think that was Tate and his crew in that explosion."

"What did he tell you?" Jimmy asked.

"Not much, just said he needed me. The son of a bitch saved my life one to many times. I owe him." His voice cracked.

His crew had never seen this side of him. They all feared him in a sense. He was the baddest son of a bitch they knew. Never had any of them seen him waver. He just shook his head and went back up on deck, leaving them sitting there looking at each other. Another hour had passed, and it was time to refuel. Stone took over the wheel while Max and the guys filled the tanks. The sky was getting lighter, so he knew they were close. Another few miles and they should be right on top of it.

Stone slowed the boat down as they approached. There was debris floating in the water. He cut the engines, the boat coming to a halt in the water. As he looked out, he could see what looked like bodies floating.

"Mother fucker," he said. "Get them out of the water. Fuck!"

The guys pulled three shredded bodies out of the water, and half of Joey. "They're all dead," one of the guys said.

"Fuck," Stone yelled and spun around. "What the fuck is going on?" Looking out in the water, he saw something orange floating low in the water. He jumped up to the wheel and started the engines, moving the boat closer. He saw two people barely floating along the surface. "There," he yelled, pointing at them. "Grab em." He cut the engines and ran to help.

They pulled Tate out of the water first, and then Stone reached over, grabbing Teresa's life jacket and pulling her up the side of the boat, into his arms. "What the fuck?" he said under his breath. Looking down at her tiny body and then at his friend, he was more than impressed that she held on to him for so long. "She is frozen. Get some warming blankets while I get her out of these clothes." He moved inside the cabin while Jones worked on Tate on deck.

Stone laid her on the bed and started removing her clothes. "Who are you, beautiful girl?" he whispered to her as he dropped the life jacket on the floor. He smiled when he saw the gun strapped to her hip. He took it off, and then her shoes, socks, and jeans came off. He pulled her jacket and shirt off. The marks and bruises from Sully were still visible. "Oh, beautiful girl, what happened to you?" Key handed him a few blankets. "Here, put one under her," he told him as he lifted her in his arms.

Key laid the blanket out. As he turned to get out of the way, he froze. "Fuck," he said. Looking at Stone. "Man, who the fuck?"

Stone looked at him. "She was fucking soaked. What the hell did you want me to do?" He'd left her in just her camisole and panties.

"No, man, look at her back. She has been whipped. Her back is sliced open," Key said as he moved.

Stone laid her down gently and rolled her over to look. "What the fuck?" He rolled her back over and wrapped the blanket around her, then lifted her in his arms and crawled into the bed, wrapping his body around her. Key stood there looking at him funny. "She's fucking freezing, asshole. Probably has hypothermia. Get Tate down here and get those fucking clothes off him. Get some more blankets and let's get the fuck out of here."

Key nodded and left. A few minutes later, the guys laid Tate, now in only his boxers, on the bed next to him and Teresa. "He's got a burn on his back and a huge lump on his head. Probably hypothermia. Let me have a look at her," Jones said.

Stone laid her on the bed next to Tate as the guys wrapped him up. Jones checked her out. "She seems unharmed except for some faded bruises and scars. What the fuck is going on, Stone?"

The boat lurched and moved across the water back to the island. "I have no fucking clue." He climbed back into the bed next to her. Get in and wrap yourself around him. We need some body heat."

Jones laughed. "Yeah, and when he wakes up and breaks my neck, I am holding you responsible."

"Yeah, let's hope he wakes up." Stone smiled. Pretty sure they looked ridiculous curled up in the bed. Two hours later, Stone and Jones got out of the bed and wrapped them together in the middle, leaving and pulling the small door closed behind them.

By the time they got back to the island, the rest of the guys had made their way there. The only one left from Tate's crew was Dev. He filled Stone in on what he was doing in New York. Stone left to make a few calls. He filled his guys in and sent everyone where they needed to be. Then he called a few more, and even made a call to his not so legal friend in Columbia.

"Anything you need, my friend. Tell me where," his friend answered.

"Chicago. No trace. Five days and I will call you," Stone said into the satellite phone.

"Done. Talk soon."

The phone went dead. Stone looked at his longtime friend and this mysterious woman lying in his arms. Jones walked up next to him. "We've got them wrapped in some electric blankets. I checked their temps and they should be good soon."

"What's going on top side? Are all the boats covered?" Stone asked as he turned to leave.

Jones turned with him. "Yeah, it's all good. Stone, what the fuck is going on?"

"I wish I knew, buddy. I wish I knew. Dev doesn't know anything. But that's how Tate works. Did you get his guys taken care of?"

"Yeah, they're on ice."

Stone nodded his head and quietly shut the door. "All we do now is wait. Try to get some shut eye."

CHAPTER NINE

Tate felt like his skin was on fire. His limbs tingled and burned like they'd been asleep, and his back felt like it had been scorched. There was a body next to him. Pulling his arm around it, he realized it was a small body. His eyes fluttered, but his head hurt like hell. When he opened his eyes, it was too dark for him to see. He raised his hand to his face; something was tickling his chin and neck. Wiping his face, he realized it was hair. But it wasn't his. Slowly turning his head, trying to force his eyes to focus, he realized the body next to his was Teresa's.

He pulled her closer to him and kissed her forehead. "Hey, beautiful," he whispered because anything louder would definitely hurt his head. He rubbed her arm. He felt her fingers move on his chest, which sent lightning through his body. "Hey," he said as she moved her head. Turning her face to his, he felt his mouth being drawn to hers.

"Are we dead?" she whispered.

Tate covered her mouth with his gently, stroking his tongue along hers. Her hand trailed up his chest to the side of his face. He pulled back and whispered, "Do you feel dead?"

Teresa giggled and shook her head. "Where are we?"

"I'm not sure. We should get up and go find out."

Tate went to move, and Teresa put her hand on his chest. "Thank you for saving me."

Tate smiled. "Good thing you put on that life jacket." He untangled himself from the blankets and slowly sat up. The pain in his head was blinding. He put his hands on the cot to steady himself. Teresa climbed out of the other side to come over and help him.

"Come on, let me help you up." She wrapped her arm under his and helped him stand.

Together, with him leaning on her just a bit, they moved to the door. Tate reached for the handle and stopped. "We have no clothes on."

Teresa started to giggle, but soon, her giggles turned to sobs. Tate felt her trembling. He wrapped an arm around her and pulled her to him. Turning, he leaned against the door for support, and together, they slid down it, Tate pulling her into his arms. "I've got you, beautiful. I've got you." He held her until her sobs subsided.

"I was in that water for so long, Tate. I wasn't sure I could hold on to you any longer. I was so scared. I couldn't do it anymore, and I closed my eyes and gave up. I remember the sky lightening as the sun cracked the horizon. I figured it was a good day to die, and I closed my eyes. I am so sorry I let you go."

"Shh, you didn't let me go. If you had, I wouldn't be here with you."

"Where is here? What if Sully got us?" She now sounded terrified.

Tate chuckled. "We wouldn't be sitting on the floor in our underwear if Sully got us. There's a light switch up there. Why don't you flip it on?"

Teresa got up and turned on the lights. It took a few minutes for their eyes to adjust. Tate chuckled. "We are at our destination."

Teresa bent down to help him up. "How do you know?"

Tate smiled at her. "Because it's my place. There should be some clothes over there in those lockers." He pointed across the room.

Teresa left him and moved to the lockers. Tate did not take his eyes off of her. He could feel himself getting hard. "Fuck," he said under his breath. Teresa came back with two pairs of sweats and two t-shirts. If she noticed his erection, she didn't say anything. They got dressed, and together, they left the room to find everyone.

Climbing the stairs took longer than he expected. "Man, my body aches," he said softly. "I took the brunt of that explosion. I wonder who else made it out. Did you see anyone?"

Teresa said in a very quiet voice, "It's just you and me who made it. The rest are gone. I'm so sorry, Tate."

He hung his head. "I figured as much." His voice was low, full of pain for the loss of his friends.

"How did we get here?" she asked as they reached the top of the stairs.

"I'm not sure, but I think I know." Tate reached for the door handle in front of him. Turning the knob, he pushed the door open. The room opened up into a cavernous space. There were tables, desks, chairs, glass walls, and computers were strewn everywhere. All the way in the back was a kitchen and a huge table, filled with men. There were men working on computers, men sleeping, men eating, men walking around wrapped in towels.

"What the fuck," Teresa whispered, more to herself than to Tate.

He squeezed her shoulder as he chuckled loud enough for one of the guys to look up. "Well, it's about fucking time your sorry ass woke up." The man pushed the chair out as he stood. Teresa watched as he stretched out in front of her. He was bigger that Tate in every way. Teresa only came up to Tate's nipple, and this man was taller still. He walked toward them, putting his hand out to grab Tate's.

"Hey, man, glad to see you made it. This is Teresa. Teresa, this is Stone."

He turned to her and smiled, running his finger down her cheek. "Hello, beautiful girl."

Teresa pulled her cheek away from him and smiled. "Hi," she said as she moved closer to Tate. Stone just smiled at her for a minute and then looked back at Tate.

"What the fuck happened out there?" Stone asked as they moved through the room. Teresa stayed very close to Tate. When they reached the table, two guys got up and Teresa and Tate sat down.

Almost immediately, plates of food were sat down in front of them, loaded high with scrambled eggs, hash browns, sausage and toast.

"Thank you," Teresa said softly as she ate and listened to Tate tell the story. He left out the detail of how Sully had tortured her. When Tate stopped talking, the room was silent. Teresa looked up, and every set of eyes was looking at her. Involuntarily, her hand started to shake. It became hard to swallow. All ears had just heard what Sully had done to her; they heard what she had done to gain her freedom. It was because of her that Tate's crew were dead. She cleared her throat and tried to speak in a normal voice, fighting the tears that were building in her eyes. "Yes, I am guilty of doing those things. But I have since done all that I can to help end this." She stood and turned to Tate. "I need a shower."

Tate nodded and began to get up, but Stone stopped him. "I've got this, buddy. You just sit and eat. I'll make sure she isn't bothered." Stone stood and put his hand out in front of him, implying she should follow him. Teresa held her head up as she made her way out of the cavernous room back to the door they came in. She followed Stone down a flight of stairs to the room where they'd been sleeping. When she walked in, Stone shut the door and locked it. Teresa turned around, looking at him. He stood in front of the door, folding his arms across his chest.

She turned her face up to his, trying not to show her fear. "What?" she spat out.

His smile scared the shit out of her. "He saved my life many times over the years. Never has he needed or asked for my help, so when he called, I came. I just pulled his crew out of the fucking lake, all of them dead. That crew helped him save me. How is it he meets you on a dark road, and two weeks later, they are all dead?" His voice was cold and hard.

Teresa stood there like a defiant child, her shoulders squared, her head held high. "I did what I had to do to save my own life. I had no clue who he was. To be honest, I really didn't give a shit. It was the only chance at my freedom. For six months, that bastard raped me and tortured me. I would have sold my own parents up the fucking

96

river to get away." A tear escaped her eye, and she wiped it away just as quickly as it fell.

"And now?" His voice was harder.

"Now, I am standing here in front of you," she snapped at him.

"Will you be an asset or a problem?"

"Apparently, I am still a problem because he blew up the fucking boat. Would you mind showing me where I can take a shower?"

Stone stepped behind her. She could feel the heat coming off his body. He didn't touch her, but he was close enough that she could feel his breath on her head as he spoke. "You are very beautiful, a siren, and that seems to have clouded his mind. But I will not hesitate to end you if I feel you are a danger to him. He stood by and watched the woman he loved die because she betrayed him. Don't think for one minute that he wouldn't do the same to you."

Teresa spun around and got in his face. "I know what he fucking did." She didn't but he didn't know that. "And I know what he is capable of, trust me. The only thing I want is to end this fucker so I can fucking go home. Now, if don't mind, I would like to take a fucking shower."

Stone was shocked that she was brave enough to stand up to him. He nodded over her shoulder to the back of the room. "The showers are over there. Towels and shampoo are there." He tilted his head to his left. "There are clean clothes in the lockers." He turned and walked out of the room, slamming the door behind him and making Teresa jump.

She stood there for what seemed like eternity, shaking, trying to calm herself down enough to move. Gathering up what she needed, she moved to the showers. There were three separate stalls. Taking her towel, she moved to the last one. Once in, she let the hot water run down her body. With all she had, she tried not to collapse. Washing her hair then her body, she placed her hands on the wall and let it come. The tears, the fear, the anger, everything just collided at once inside her and, she couldn't hold it back anymore. *How did my life become this? How am I surviving? I should be dead, along with his crew.* Her silent tears became sobs. Her legs started to shake, which brought her to her knees.

Tate came in the room and heard the water running. He didn't want to intrude in her space, so he grabbed some clean clothes and went to leave to go upstairs to shower. But he thought he heard a noise and moved toward the showers. The closer he got, the louder the sound. He could hear her crying, sobbing behind the sound of the water. Without thinking, he pulled off his shirt and dropped his sweats and moved toward her cries. When he reached the last stall, he found her kneeling on the floor with her hand over her mouth, her body shaking and heaving from the torrent of sobs coming from within her. Without thinking about the fact that he was in his boxers and she was naked, he moved into the stall, dropping to his knees, and wrapped his arms around her. Teresa flinched and freaked out, trying to get away from him, throwing herself into the corner. The terrified face that looked up at him ripped his heart out.

"Oh, beautiful, I am not going to hurt you," he said softly.

Teresa moved like lightning and was in his arms, knocking him down on his ass in a flash. His arms felt like they were home as he wrapped them around her tiny body, pulling her to him. He didn't expect his body to react the way it did, feeling her beautiful pale skin pressed against his chest. He held her close to him while she continued to sob.

With jagged breaths, she said, "I'm so scared."

"I've got you." He tried to keep his body in check. There was no way he could get hard right now; she would definitely freak out. But his reaction to her was outweighing his practical mind. Her arms pulled tighter around his neck, and she pulled her head up to rest on his shoulder. God, she felt incredible in his arms. Her wet body against his, he held her. As she calmed down, Teresa, pulled back a bit. Tate loosened his arms around her. They were inches apart, her chest just barely touching his.

Swallowing hard, Tate said in a whispered voice, "Beautiful."

Without thinking, Teresa pressed her mouth against his, trailing her tongue lightly over his top lip, before opening her mouth to fully kiss him. Tate was instantly hard. A low growl moved up from deep in his chest as he kissed her back. It started out slow and tender. As each moment passed, the intensity grew and their passion built. Tate moved his hands from her back up to hold her face, his hand nearly as big as her head. Needing to slow it down, reluctantly, he pulled back, putting his forehead on hers while they got their breathing under control. This woman in his arms had been brutally raped and tortured. She was so fragile and terrified. Taking this any further would only damage her more. Tate could be rough; hell, he preferred it rough, and God knew he wanted to slam into her sweet body and take what he wanted from her. But it would only make him a monster. What he felt for her was far more than his own self-gratification. Hell, he couldn't figure out where his mind crossed the line. He couldn't let her in. He couldn't get close to her, not like this, not until this mess was all settled. Not until he was sure it wasn't just the moment they were in. Fear had a way of doing things to people, making them do things they usually regretted, and he knew there was no way he wanted her to regret him.

"This cannot happen, beautiful," he whispered, his pain evident in his voice.

"You don't want me?" He heard the pain in her voice. "How could you?" She moved to get up. Standing, she reached for a towel to cover herself with. "No one will ever want me again. He has destroyed my body, my mind, my soul." She ran out of the shower and into the room, stopping in the middle of the room when she realized Stone was standing at the door.

Tate was right behind her. "Leave," he said to Stone.

"What the fuck are you doing, Tate?" he barked back, making Teresa jump.

"I said to fucking leave!" Tate yelled, staring him down.

Stone turned and walked out, slamming the door behind him. Tate walked up to Teresa to stand in front of her. "You think I don't want you?"

She was crying again, as she nodded her head.

"Look at me," Tate said.

She turned around and screamed, "Just leave me alone. Go, just go."

Tate was pissed. "No!" he shouted. "No, I am tired of these fucking emotions fucking up my head."

She spun around. Tate took a step back. The fire in her eyes was a bit more than he expected. This tiny woman held more conviction than any other woman he had ever met in his life. "Emotions, you want to talk about emotions? I'll tell you about emotions. Fear! Now, there's an emotion. For the past six to seven months, I have known fear like you can only ever fucking dream of knowing. Anger. That's a fucking emotion I know well. It runs in my fucking veins. It's thicker than the blood I have in my body. How about hatred? That's a big emotion!" She was screaming.

Tate grabbed her and covered her mouth before she could continue. She responded to him, kissing him back. Tate jerked her back. "Exactly why this can't continue. Beautiful, don't you see what you do to me?" He looked down at his erection.

Her eyes followed his. "Uh," she whispered.

"I can't do this with you. You have been through so much. What you're feeling is not who you are. I know, I've done the same thing many times. It's a knee jerk reaction to the myriad of emotions that are flooding through you. I am not going to be the one to hurt you again." He lowered his voice. "I like it rough sometimes, especially when I'm feeling the way I am right now. I would only hurt you. Hell, beautiful, you haven't even healed yet. So, don't think for one minute that I don't want you."

Teresa swallowed hard. Not sure her voice would work, she whispered, "How do you feel right now?"

Tate chuckled. "Like I want to spend a week, hell, a lifetime tasting every inch of your body." Teresa inhaled deeply. "I feel like, once I start, I will never be able to stop. Don't for one minute think I don't want you. When you are healed, when this is over... If we are still alive, maybe. But nothing is going to happen until we end that fucking bastard. Okay?"

Teresa pulled her bottom lip between her teeth and nodded,

looking deep into his eyes. She knew the words he spoke were the truth. She knew from the size of that erection in his pants that he wanted her a lot.

"Now, I am going to take a shower, so you can get dressed. If you want, go up top, and I'll meet you there. If not, I should be out in a minute." He moved around her and headed for the showers. Teresa turned to watch him walk away. She couldn't help but smile. He was magnificent, scars and all. Once he turned into the showers, she went to the lockers and grabbed some clothes. There were smaller sizes, so she grabbed those. At least, they didn't make her feel like she was a child.

There was a knock on the door, and she yelled, "Come in."

Stone walked into the room carrying her clothes. "One of the guys thought you might want these back."

"Thank you," she said, taking the folded clothes from him and putting them on one of the cots.

"Listen, I need to apologize to you," Stone began.

Tate was coming out of the shower and stopped just short of the doorway.

"You don't need to apologize. I understand where you're coming from, and I don't blame you. I wouldn't trust me, either, if I were in your shoes."

Stone chuckled. "I need you to know, in a non-offensive way, that I won't hesitate."

She put her hand up. "Same here." She looked him square in the eyes.

He smiled, walking up to her. He reached up and ran his finger down her cheek. "Then we understand one another, beautiful girl."

Teresa pushed his hand away and took a step back. "Don't fucking touch me again, and don't call me beautiful. My name is Teresa."

Stone busted out laughing. From the corner of his eye, he saw Tate come around the corner. Turning to him, he said, "I like her. She has spunk. We need to talk up top." Turning to Teresa, he said, "Alone." Then he turned and left the room.

Teresa sat down on the cot and put her head in her hands, while

Tate got dressed. He sat down on one across from her while he put on some boots. "You alright?" he asked.

"I will be." She looked up at him. "He's a bit full of himself."

Tate chuckled. "He's one of the most honorable men I know. A bit shady but honorable." Teresa nodded her head. Tate lifted his hand to run his finger down her cheek and stopped midair. She looked at it, then at him. She saw a bit of worry in his eyes and immediately reached for his hand. Pulling it to her mouth, she gently kissed his fingers then let it go. "Why don't you go across to the weight room? There is work out equipment in there. Try to get your strength back. I am sure it will be empty. I'll come find you when I am done."

"I think I might just sleep."

Tate nodded and then got up, moving to the door. He turned as he opened it to see her curling up with her back to him. She pulled a pillow into her arms. He walked through and closed the door behind him. Halfway up the stairs, he stopped. Something wasn't right. They hadn't finished their conversation. She hadn't finished what she needed to say to him. He turned around and went back to the room. When he opened the door, he saw her shoulders shaking. He closed his eyes. God, he hated when a woman cried. Shaking his head, he gently closed the door and walked over to the cot. He laid down and pulled her to him.

"What is wrong, beautiful?"

Teresa turned, and he pulled her to his chest while she sobbed. She finished crying and pulled away from him, climbing off the cot to sit on the one next to it. Tate sat up.

"I think all that has happened has finally hit me. When I sat up there and listened to you tell those men what had happened, it was like I had a slight reprieve from the chaos. It was very overwhelming. Then coming down here and finally having a few minutes to myself, it kind of all came running at me. You don't know me. You don't know anything about me. I am not this woman, this person. I was strong and independent. I feared nothing or no one. Then fucking Sully and that bastard Ted did this to me."

"It's called conditioning," Tate said softly.

"I know what it is. I am not some stupid insipid girl. My point is, I can't seem to get control. All those men up there scare the shit out of me. You may think you know what that bastard did to me from my injuries, but you don't have a clue what he did to my mind. I am so fucked up right now. Stone is probably right; I am a danger for you. You should have killed me back at the house."

Tate smiled. "Come on." Standing, he put his hand out, waiting for her to take it. When she did, he pulled her off the cot and walked her across the hall. He pushed open the door and pulled her into a room filled with work out equipment. There were a few guys lifting weights, and two were sparring in a makeshift ring. There was one guy hitting and kicking a bag, while another guy held it in place. "Excuse me, guys, could we have a minute?" he asked. There were nods all around, and everyone left. "You need to work this out. Kick the bag, hit the bag, run, do whatever you need to do. I will help you, or I can have one of the guys who isn't so scary help you out. But if you say you are this woman, or were this woman, then here is the place you can find her again. Or at least get all this pent-up anger out. We have a serious job to do, and if you are going to go off half-cocked and get yourself killed, then I am going to have to leave you here when we leave." Teresa opened her mouth to say something, but Tate put his finger over her lips. "Do this for yourself, beautiful."

She pulled her head away. "Why do you call me that?"

Tate smiled. "Because you are." It was the simple truth. "Now, I have a meeting to get to." He turned toward the door. "Jacobs," he yelled out. A guy came trotting over. "Jacobs, this is Teresa. She has some issues she needs to work out. Would you mind taking her under your wing and keep her sane." He leaned in and said just loud enough for Teresa to hear, "She's a bit emotional."

Teresa hit him and he laughed.

"Not a problem, Tate. Nice to meet you, Teresa."

She nodded to him. Tate kissed her on the forehead. "I need to go. I'll be upstairs if you need me. I will be back later."

Tate left Teresa to work out her frustrations. Climbing the stairs, he found himself smiling. What a hell of a time to smile. All hell was about to break loose and he was smiling.

Walking into the communications room, Stone looked at him with a look that could only mean trouble. "What's going on?"

Stone just stared at him. "Before we start all of this, I need to clear the air here. What is your relationship with Teresa?"

Tate chuckled. "I told you. I saved her and hell came down on us."

"Well, it looks like you are more involved than that. Tate, man, she held on to you for hours in that water. How is that possible? She can't weigh but a hundred pounds if that. There is something more here, and I need to know if your emotions are going to get in the way."

Tate was pissed. "Listen to me. My relationship or non-relation-ship with her is not up for discussion, and it certainly is none of your fucking business. The mother fucker who has taken down my entire crew is my fucking step-father. The fucker killed my mother and raped my sister. I thought I killed the bastard fifteen years ago, but apparently, I failed. With or without your fucking help, I will not fail again."

Stone smiled. "There you are." He slapped Tate on the back. "Now, let's get down to some business."

Tate nodded. "What do you know?"

"We've been monitoring Dev's cameras, and we got a whole lot. He is trafficking women. From what we can tell, mostly young girls. I am sure a few, if not more, are under aged girls. I sent twenty guys to New York. They have arrived and are set up to intervene and to stop the sale of as many as they can. The loss of life on this is going to grow. Now, I called my buddy in Columbia."

Tate's eyes widened. He knew the guy. He was the kind of guy who left no witnesses and took no prisoners. The man was ruthless.

"Yeah, once I saw the boat, I knew we didn't have a choice. A crew of fifty or more are on their way to Chicago. Five days and we can begin our take-down of this guy."

"No one kills him. He is mine and Teresa's."

Stone nodded. "So, we have five days to get our shit together. I have guys going through the hall of records down there. We will find every fucking building the fucker owns, and we will have the blue-prints for them all. What does your girl know?"

"She knows a great deal. I had all the files on the boat. I'm pretty sure you'll be able to duplicate them all. She is ex-F.B.I. She has a great deal of training and is a Special Investigative ADA. She is smart and knows her shit. She did some undercover work into Sully and his business. Apparently, she gathered enough information to go to the Grand Jury for an indictment. Her boyfriend, a Detective Ted Hardt, is in Sully's pocket. Apparently, he sat and watched while Sully tortured her and raped her. I still don't know how she survived six months of what he did to her. She is still healing."

"I saw the marks on her when I stripped her after we pulled the two of you out of the lake. She was pretty beaten up, huh?"

Tate nodded. "I still can't believe she survived. She is a tough woman."

"Listen, man, we've known each other for a long time. Don't let her damsel in distress persona hinder your objective. She has to be just another case, man, or you could get us all killed."

"I know. Kelly said the same thing to me before we left. This all needs to be taken care if in twenty-one days. Kelly and Taylor are locked in the safe room at my place in Arlington. She has twenty-one days' worth of food remaining. I left her there because, if Sully gets his hands on her, he will force me to watch as he rapes her and Taylor, and then he will kill them both."

"Don't worry, it will be over long before then. So, Teresa is F.B.I. Do you mind if I have her checked out?"

Tate laughed. "Like you haven't already."

"Of course, I did. Just thought I would be courteous."

That brought Tate into a roaring laugh. "You courteous? Now, that is hilarious. So, what did you find out?"

"Well, she was a top agent. She is highly intelligent. She has nothing but top scores on every fucking test or exam they have. The side notes in her file from her instructors are all the same. She is and would be a valuable asset to any team. So, she has excellent training. She is the youngest Special Investigative ADA in the history of

Chicago, and she has a hell of a future putting away bad guys like you and me. You sure you know what you're doing here, Tate?"

Tate laughed. "To be honest, I don't have a fucking clue, but when I saw her fight that man while he beat her, she didn't give up until he knocked her out. Something in me changed. When I picked her up off that street, her tiny beaten body, something inside of me snapped. Then when I saw her back, I was instantly filled with rage. The idea that he has been doing this to woman for the past fifteen years makes my blood boil. I'll be fine, and when it's done, I will take her to her family. Then, I'll get my sister and my niece and I am out. I'm done. I've got enough money to live out five lifetimes."

Stone nodded. "Yeah, I think I'm too old for this shit. I might follow you."

They all sat around and worked on a plan. Hours of pouring over reports and information, listening in on conversations and watching monitors.

Teresa was still working out with Jacobs when Tate finished and came looking for her. He stood in the doorway watching her beat the shit out of the bag. Jacobs was holding strong, but they guy looked beat. Tate chuckled and walked over to relieve him. "Hey, man, I've got this," he said.

Jacobs looked at him and smiled. "The girl has a bunch of energy. She's pretty tough."

Teresa smiled at him. "Lots of anger," she said as the guys switched places. She didn't stop, she just beat the hell out of the bag. Tate found himself behind her thrusts and kicks. He couldn't wipe the smile off his face. She was moving him back with each kick to the bag. After another ten minutes or so, she stopped. "I think I'm going to be sore in the morning."

"Come on, I'll rub you down. We have some mentholated rub here. Get changed and meet me in the steam room." He nodded toward a door on the far side of the room. "I'll change into some shorts. There should be something in there that will fit you."

Teresa nodded and moved to the steam room. She put on a pair of shorts and a t-shirt, then went in and laid on the bed on her stomach.

Tate came in a few minutes later. He started with her legs, rubbing and massaging the menthol deep into her limbs.

He found himself getting aroused as he moved up to her thighs. She was so tiny, his hands fitting all the way around her thigh. As he pushed up her shorts, his fingers caressed the bottom of her ass, his index finger barely brushing her center. He groaned inwardly as he tried to focus. When he finished with her legs, he was rock hard. He had heard the little mews and groans from her, and it just fueled him more. He moved to her arms and shoulders. It was difficult with the shirt on to achieve maximum penetration, but he knew if he asked her to take off her shirt, he would have to touch more of her soft, alabaster skin, and that would be a huge mistake.

"There, that should do it." His voice came out sounding groggy. He wiped his hands clean with a damp towel before tossing it into the corner.

Teresa rolled over onto her back and looked at him with wanton eyes. He could see her pupils were dilated. She licked her lips, and her eyes moved down his sweat-laden body to his more than obvious erection. With a shaky hand, she slowly reached out and gently caressed him. Her tiny hand gently stroked the outline of his cock. He closed his eyes at the marvelous sensation running through his body. He couldn't do this; he was going to explode right there in his shorts. He stepped back, taking her hand in his. "God, beautiful, what are you doing?"

She sat up, and then got on her knees on the table so they were eye to eye. "I don't know what is happening or why it's happening, but every time I am near you, my body seems to come alive. I thought this part of me was dead. I learned to not feel anything while I was with Sully."

Tate tried to speak in his normal voice, but lust had taken control of him. "Listen, we cannot act on this. I will not compromise you. My body desires you. My God, who wouldn't? You are perfect and beautiful, and this mouth," he reached up and ran his thumb across her lips, "is perfection. I can't think straight."

"Then don't," she said.

It happened so fast; he grabbed her around the neck with his other hand and smashed his mouth to hers. Pulling her against him, his erection pressed on her stomach. The kiss was deep and passionate, but he ended it as quickly as he started it. "You are a siren for me. This cannot happen again until our job is finished. Then, if you still think you want this, we will talk. I am here to protect you and to help you gain your freedom so you can go home to your family. Nothing more. When this is over, I am done with this job, with this line of work. You, my beautiful girl, are my last job." He pulled away and walked out of the room, leaving her sitting on her haunches.

Teresa smiled and touched her lips. She climbed off the table and made her way back to the room where all the cots were. She went to grab her clothes and then headed to the showers. One of the stalls was running, so she went into another one and pulled the curtain. Getting out of her clothes, she turned on the shower and let the hot water run over her body. When she finished, she grabbed a towel for her hair and then one for her body. Without thinking, simply because her mind was still on that kiss, and the way he felt in her hand, she pulled open the curtain. Standing not five feet from her with his back to her was Tate. She gasped as she took in his body. Every part of it was muscle, ripples of muscles all the way down his back, even his ass and legs. He was beautiful.

He turned to look at her, grabbing a towel to cover himself. Teresa licked her lips, drawing her bottom one into her mouth and looked into his eyes. "You are so beautiful," she whispered.

Tate smiled. Picking up his clothes, he walked past her. Leaning in, he said, "I think you have that wrong. You are the one that is beautiful." He kissed her on the forehead and walked out of the shower room.

Teresa watched him leave, marveling at the muscles rippling as he walked out. Letting out a breath she wasn't aware of holding, she picked up her clothes and got dressed.

Tate was waiting for her when she came out. "Let's get something to eat. We have a few more days before we leave here. I want Jones to have a look at those cuts on your back. We spent a great deal of time in the water, and I don't want you to get sick, or an infection."

Teresa nodded and they made their way up to the control room. While they ate, Stone questioned her about what information or insight she might have that could help. It was many hours before they were finished and Teresa went to get up to leave. "I think you should camp out up here in one of the private rooms. These guys need to get some shut eye, and well, I'm sure you don't want to sleep in the same place as them."

She blushed. "Thank you. Where should I go?"

Tate stood. "Come on, I'll get you settled." She followed him to the back of the room, past the kitchen and down a hall. There were several doors, but he led her to the door at the very end of the hallway. "This is my room. You can stay in here."

"Where are you going to sleep?" she asked softly as he opened the door.

"I'll bunk with the guys. I'll check on you before I go down."

She nodded and turned as he was leaving. He smiled at her and closed the door, leaving her alone in the room. The bed was not what she expected to see in an underground command center. It was a huge king-sized bed sitting in the middle of the room. To her left was a door. She opened it, finding a private bathroom with a shower. Smiling, she shut the door and climbed into the bed. She was tired, so falling asleep was easy. Keeping the dreams, well, nightmares away was another thing all together.

Teresa woke to complete darkness, screaming at the top of her lungs. The door flew open, and Stone came running in, flipping on the lights. Teresa was curled up in a ball with her knees drawn up to her chin in the corner of the bed, shaking and crying. Stone moved with great swiftness and gathered her up in his arms, pulling her close to his chest.

"I've got you," he whispered. "I've got you."

Teresa tried to pull away from him, but he wouldn't let go. "Please," she said. "Just don't touch me." Stone let her go, and she crawled off the bed and went to the corner of the room. "Please, just leave me alone," she sobbed.

"Sweetheart, I am not going to hurt you," Stone said softly.

"Just, please," she cried.

Stone nodded and got up to walk to the door. "Do you want me to get Tate?"

Her head turned to look at him. He saw panic rise in them as she shook her head. "I just want to be left alone. These are my demons," she whispered. He shut the door and left her. Trembling, Teresa climbed back into the bed, grabbing the pillow and clutching it to her chest, and cried herself back to sleep.

It wasn't long before they began again. This time when she woke, she got up and wandered to the workout room and began punching and kicking the bag. By the time Tate found her, her hands were a bloody mess.

He grabbed her and pulled her away. "Let me go!" she screamed at him.

"Look at your hands, Teresa." He tried to calm her down.

"I don't fucking care. I need to do this. I need to get him out of my head. I can't go on like this." She pushed on Tate to release her. But he just held her tighter. "Please, just let me go. Stop trying to save me. You can't make it stop. No one can." Her voice quivered.

"Teresa, look at me."

"No!" she yelled. "Let me go!"

Tate grabbed her face and slammed his mouth over hers, kissing her. She struggled and fought against him, but after a few moments, she calmed down. Her hands moved up around his neck, her fingers threading through his thick hair. She lifted herself up his body. Tate put his hands on her ass, and she wrapped her legs around his waist. She weighed nothing to him. Their kiss was frenzied and fueled with lust and desire. His cock hardened when she bit into his bottom lip.

He pulled back. "Ah, beautiful, I am not going to be able to stop."

"Then don't, Tate. I need to feel alive again. I need to know I can feel anything but this fear that has consumed me for so long. I need..."

He cut her off with his kiss. He was moving out the door, up the stairs, across the command center, the whole time kissing her. A few of the guys just watched in silence as he carried her, the passion and desire evident to them. Down the hall and through the doors, he carried her into his room. He turned and bolted the door and walked to the bed, holding her as he laid her down.

Slowly, they undressed one another. She lay on her back while he hovered over her. He sat back on his heels to look at her. "You are so fucking beautiful," he whispered. He could see her chest heave from her deep breaths. He bent down to kiss her sweetly, the hunger tamed for now. He enjoyed her mouth, her neck, his mouth working its way down her chest. Gently, his hands moved from her hips up her sides, brushing his thumbs along the bottom of her breasts. Teresa arched her back, pushing her already erect nipples up to his mouth.

His warm breath danced across her left nipple, causing her to moan. They were beautiful, perfectly taut and ready for him. His desire to feel one roll across his tongue was too much for him, and he couldn't wait another minute to taste one. When his lips touched her, she cried out, "Oh God!" Then he drew it into the warmth of his mouth and gently sucked it, pinching it between his teeth, sending her over the edge. Tate could feel her body convulse with pleasure, and she shook and rode out her orgasm. He sucked and tasted it until she was finished, and then moved onto the next one. Again, she responded in like. She was jelly under his touch.

"Please, Tate," she moaned.

"Oh, beautiful, I have just begun. You want to feel. I am going to make you feel." He groaned and moved down her stomach, kissing her skin, kissing every scar, every bruise, loving her with his mouth, drawing in her sweet scent. When he reached her hairline, her back arched off the bed, pushing her hips down away from his mouth. "Do you want me to stop, beautiful?"

She shook her head, simply because she couldn't speak. Tate smiled as he buried his face in her full mound of hair and took a deep breath. "You smell incredible." He moved, half-laying on the bed between her legs. Slowly and gently, she opened herself to him. With his fingers, he opened her wider to find what he was looking for.

There she was, her swollen little bud waiting for him. He moved close, jetting his tongue out to touch her. Her hips bucked off the bed, and Tate moved his hand up to press down on her stomach, holding her in place as his mouth covered her and gently suckled her bud. She tasted so sweet to him. She felt incredible on his tongue. He kissed her there, and then flattened his tongue against her clit and gently swirled it around. Her hips moved in slow circles with him. Teresa could do nothing but lay there and feel his desire, feel the ecstasy he was bringing her. She brought her fingers up to push through his hair so lovingly, and he could feel them tighten against his scalp as she started to climax.

"Oh God, Tate," she whispered as she came undone. Her hands went lax as her body shuddered underneath him.

He could feel her pulse as she came, wave after wave. He moved his head and opened his mouth, taking every pulse of orgasm she had, running his tongue along the length of her. When he'd taken it all, he moved up her body. Looking into her eyes, he saw what he needed to see, her complete submission to him. She would do anything for him, and yet he wanted nothing from her, which was something entirely new to him.

She reached up and touched his cheek, gently pulling him down to her mouth and kissing him as he slowly entered her. He was huge, so he took it slow. Inch by inch, he moved deeper and deeper. Their kiss became more intense the further he moved. She was so tight against him, he nearly came and had to stop so he could get his wits about him. She felt like silk wrapped around him. Then he moved again until he was buried balls deep inside of her. They kissed while she stretched to accommodate him. Pulling back to look into her eyes again, he noticed the tears on her face.

"Am I hurting you?" he asked softly.

She shook her head. "No, I feel again. I feel pleasure and joy. Not pain," she assured him, her voice soft.

Tate kissed her and started moving, slowly fucking her. Her moans were absorbed into his mouth, her hands moving over his back and ass. Tate felt her nails press into his back, and he felt her tighten around him. She was going to come again, and if she did, he was gone. She felt incredible to him, so perfect. The way she hugged his cock was like nothing he'd ever felt before, and then her back arched and her chest pressed into his and she let go, contracting around him. As she pulsed around him, he couldn't hold on any longer. He pushed one more time and exploded deep inside of her. Kissing her hard, they shook and climaxed together.

As they calmed down, her hold on him tightened. He rolled onto his side, bringing her with him so he could hold her. He noticed she was shaking. "Hey, are you all right?" He kissed her forehead.

Teresa nodded. "Thank you."

"You don't need to thank me." He pulled her closer.

She took in a breath and shuddered. Tate pulled back, bringing his finger up to her chin and lifting her face to meet his. "What's going on in that beautiful head of yours?"

"Why did you do this? You said we couldn't." She sounded accusatory.

"I did this because you made me feel that you needed this to begin to heal. I did this because I couldn't stand not doing this anymore."

She got up and sat on the bed next to him. "You kissed every mark on my body. Was this a pity thing? Do you feel sorry for me? Did you do this because you thought you could take advantage of me?"

Tate sat up. "Don't ever think that way. You have no clue the kind of man I am. I can't believe you would think I would take advantage of you. I know this was a mistake. This was the worst thing I could have ever done. But I did it, and I take full responsibility for it. If you want to think I took advantage of you, that's fine. I can't do anything about that." He got up and grabbed his pants, putting them on and then his shirt. "I am still going after Sully, with or without you. It isn't just about you." He leaned down and got right in her face. "That mother fucker murdered my mother and raped my little sister. So, if you think for one minute I just did what I did for anything other than I wanted you, then that shit is on you, not me. I didn't use a condom, so I will see if Jones has that morning after pill so you don't have to worry about getting pregnant." He pulled away and stormed to the door.

As he jerked it open, he heard her say, "He made sure I can't have children."

Tate froze, closing his eyes. A flash of her stomach came to his mind. Matching scars on either side of her hips. He turned around to see her tiny body, with her knees drawn up to her chest, sitting on the edge of the bed. He closed the door and moved to kneel in front of her.

"What did he do?" he asked in a whisper.

"He had my ovaries removed. They didn't give me any anesthetic. He told me it was punishment for breaking his nose."

She was in his arms before she could take a breath. "Oh my God, beautiful. I am so sorry. I am so sorry." She started to cry. "I cannot even begin to imagine the things you endured."

"He always made sure I healed, and then he would start all over again. He told me I wasn't going to ever need them, and he certainly didn't want any snot-nosed bastards running around."

Tate rocked back and forth with her in his arms, holding her and comforting her. He pulled the sheet off the bed to cover her with, to help her feel safe. She cried herself to sleep in his arms. His hold didn't waiver, just like the night in the lake when she held on to him to save his life. She needed him now and he wasn't going to fail her.

He must have fallen asleep himself, because someone had opened the door and the light had crossed his eyes. Teresa was still wrapped in his arms asleep. Somehow, he managed to stand up and lay her in the bed. He stood over her, looking at the very broken woman in his bed. He fucked up crossing that line. Something was terribly wrong with him. He had never done anything like this. He'd made love to her the night before, and he had never done that before. He smiled, thinking about it. It was incredible, the way he felt, the way she felt. But he still couldn't shake the feeling that it was something more.

He left the room and went up top to get some fresh air. Stone was standing on the edge of the dock, so he walked out there.

"You crossed a line last night. You know that, right? You fucked up," he said to him.

"I know. I don't know what happened. But I can't undo it. To be honest, I don't want to. She got to me."

"What if that is the plan? What if she is supposed to seduce you? He had her for six months, Tate. She could be programmed. We need to be very careful here. I can't let her come on this mission. She is a threat and you know it."

Tate swallowed hard. He did know it. "I suppose I knew it all along. Maybe that's why I did what I did. She's fucked up big time. That bastard tortured her. He removed her ovaries without any anesthetic."

Stone looked at him. "That's fucked up. I'm sorry about all of this, but she is a threat. You called me for help. I had no idea she was the issue."

"In the beginning, she was. But then I figured out who he was, and it is no longer about her and what happened to her. This bastard killed my mother and raped Kelly. She was just a little girl. He nearly killed her then. He has to be stopped. He is now after Kelly's daughter, and I will die before I let anything happen to her."

Stone laughed. "You are dead already. He has no idea you survived that explosion. Listen, I called my buddy down in Columbia. We have two days left and then it's on. We've already taken out four guys and rescued six girls in New York. This guy Sully, he knows we are coming for him. I've got guys on him in Chicago, and he's moving shop. He won't get far, but we leave here tomorrow night. It's a done deal. When this is over, Tate, you need to disappear, and you need to take Kelly and Taylor with."

"Yeah, with my guys all gone, I'm out anyway. I'm getting too old for this shit." He chuckled.

"I know what you mean. Listen, I came into your room for a reason. We uncovered some sensitive information. Only me, Jones, and Key know. But I think you should be aware of what is really going on." Stone handed Tate a piece of paper.

He opened it and read what was on it. "Fuck."

"I'm not sure how any of this fits with what you've told me, but he's been on the payroll for as long as he has been married to Kelly. I think it was an inside job to gain information on you."

"Are you fucking kidding me?"

"Yeah, no, so wherever you have her stashed, my suggestion is you leave her there."

"What else do you know? How far does this go?"

"It goes all the way to Columbia. But my buddy isn't into under-aged girls. He just likes them submissive. So, he has agreed to end his association with your friend, and to end him. My buddy has a four-teen-year-old daughter. He said just the thought of it happening to her makes his blood boil. He is doing this one favor for me, no strings attached. Are you ready to burn down the house?"

Tate looked at Stone. "Give me the fucking match." He crumbled the paper and handed it to Stone, walking away. He made his way to the exercise room, put on some gloves, and started beating the bag. He didn't stop until a hand touched his arm. Mid-swing he turned to face Teresa. "You need to leave me alone right now," he snapped at her and swung again at the bag. She backed up and left, going back to his room.

Tate felt like a shithead, but he couldn't let that stop him. He needed to focus. He needed to get his head on straight or he stood a very good chance of getting killed. He had trust issues as it was, and now, he needed to face this shit with her head on. She had to have known that James was in this. She had to have known. Tate beat the bag for a while longer, trying to get his temper under control, but it wasn't helping. He threw off the gloves and made his way upstairs. He had no other choice but to confront her, to find out the truth. Was she still in this with Sully? Was her job to ultimately seduce him?

Making his way upstairs, he stormed into the control room, bee-lining to his room. Teresa was sitting at the table eating with a few of the guys and Stone. She had a pretty little smile on her face, and they were laughing about something. Tate walked right up to the table across from her, slamming his hands down, causing the room to grow very silent. He waited for her to look up at him. When their eyes met, he said, "What was your directive when Sully let you go?"

"I told you," she said defiantly.

"Tell me again!" Tate snapped.

"I was to lead him to you, then lead you away, to leave Kelly unprotected."

"Bullshit!" he screamed at her.

Stone sat there watching her reaction to his friend. He never expected Tate to react the way he did.

Teresa squared her shoulders and got up. "I fucking told you everything I know."

It happened so fast; Tate grabbed her by the front of her shirt and pulled her across the table right up to his face. "You are a fucking liar. Now, tell me everything!"

"Or what? You going to hurt me, Tate?" she screamed at him.

His blood was boiling. She was fucking playing with him. None of what happened between them meant anything. Before he realized what he was doing, she was sailing through the air. He had thrown her across the room. Teresa hit the floor pretty hard and slid about ten feet. Tate was right behind her. She managed to get on her feet, and when he came after her, she fought back, splitting his lip and bringing him to his knees when she kicked him in the balls.

She took off running while he was down, but he managed to grab her leg, making her fall hard to the floor. He scrambled around with her on the floor. She got in a few more good hits, and another knee to the groin. But Tate managed to pin her down.

"Get off me," she screamed.

"Tell me?"

"Get the fuck off me."

"Tate," Stone said.

"Stay the fuck out of this," he snapped at him.

"Tate, you do realize you have a hundred-pound woman pinned under your body. Let her up, she can't go anywhere."

Trying to calm himself down, he realized Stone was right and he climbed off her. Teresa scrambled to get up. She noticed a fork lying on the floor, picked it up, and slammed it in his thigh. "Touch me again and I will fucking kill you," she spat out as she bolted to his room and slammed the door.

Tate looked down at the fork buried in his thigh. "Fuck! Are you fucking kidding me?" He grunted as he pulled it out and threw it on the floor.

Stone chuckled. "That one has a bit of life to her. You should be careful, buddy. I think she just about kicked your ass."

Tate got up and headed toward his room. Reaching for the handle only to discover it was locked, it took one kick and the door flew open. Teresa was pacing the room when the door flew opened, and she charged him.

"Fucking bastard," she screamed. He caught her mid-swing and wrapped his arms around her. "Let me fucking go."

He squeezed tighter. "No fucking way, you will talk to me and you will tell me what I want to know. What was your objective, Teresa?"

"I fucking told you. Now, let me go. Just fucking let me go."

Tate dropped her on her ass and walked out of the room. He was so pissed he punched the wall on his way out. He punched the wall again on his way out of the command center. He headed up top, needing to run off this anger, needing to get his head on straight. Pushing open the door, the cool morning air hit him hard. It was chilly, but he didn't care. Slamming the door, he headed out to the woods. The island was big but not big enough to do any serious damage to his lungs. He had over the years ran a path in the ground. A bit overgrown, since he hadn't been here for some time, but it was still visible. He set his pace hard and kept at it. Hours had passed and a soft mist of rain had begun. He needed to get his head on straight. In less than twenty-four hours, they were off to Chicago to end this shit. Hopefully, Kelly and Taylor were doing fine. He had a satellite phone he could call her on, but who the hell knew what kind of equipment Sully had. The son of a bitch seemed to be very well connected.

James kept popping into his head, how and why he fucking would do this shit. Was he in on it the whole time? Did Sully find something to black mail him with? Did Sully find Kelly and use that against

James? And the biggest question: why hadn't he seen it or felt it? What had gotten into him over the years? What the fuck was he thinking, sleeping with Teresa? She was so fucking beautiful, and so sweet to taste and to feel. Had it been that long since a woman intrigued him, made his senses go off? God, the feel of her skin on his fingers, the way she was so responsive to him, the sweet nectar that she emanated from that beautiful pussy of hers. "What the fuck." He growled and continued running.

This was all so fucked up. Maybe he should have Stone beat the shit out of him. He chuckled. Yeah, he would love that.

Hours passed, and his legs were burning. He was nowhere near calm so he headed back in. He needed a shower and some food. As he came around the last bend in the trail and headed toward the door he noticed someone sitting on the edge of the dock. The tiny body let him know it was Teresa. He was too angry to say anything so he just nodded to Jacobs, who was standing at the door keeping an eye on her, and went down to take a shower.

Stone was waiting for him. "You done now?"

"For now, why? What's up?"

Stone laughed. "You attempt to beat the shit out of a woman, who is two hundred pounds lighter than you, she hands you your ass, and then you spend three and a half hours pounding the pavement. What the fuck is going on with you? We've known each other a long fucking time, and I have never seen you so unfocused."

Tate looked at his friend. "I don't know what fuck is happening to me. I am so confused and fucking worried about Kelly. Sully, well Frank, is one sick fucker. I still can't believe Teresa survived that shit."

"Hey, man, it's obvious to everyone that you have it bad for her, but this guy, he conditions these women to do as they are told. She was there for six months; you have no clue about her mental state. She could just be a program waiting to unwind."

"I know, man. Don't I fucking know it. I can't seem to stay away from her, and I don't think that's programming. From the minute I picked her up off that fucking street, I felt drawn to her. I can't explain it, and I think that's the thing that pisses me off the most is that she is fucking playing me. I barely survived Jenny."

"We were all there with you, man. I know what you went through. But this time, you have your eyes wide open. You know what happened. Tate, man, you need to be careful with her. You threw that girl across the room. Jones looked her over, no broken bones, but take it easy on her. She is a woman, for fuck's sake."

"Yeah, I know. I need to apologize."

"No, I am the one to apologize," Teresa said from the doorway. "I baited you on purpose for rejecting me in the weight room."

Stone looked from her to him. "Listen, I am going to leave you two to figure this shit out. We've got twenty-four hours before wheels up. Get your shit together."

Tate nodded and watched Stone leave the room. Then his glare switched to Teresa. They stood there looking at one another. Tate shook his head, turned, and headed for the showers, undressing as he went. He was still too angry to talk. Turning on the water, placed his hands against the wall, letting it run over him.

It was the feel of her tiny silken hands on his chest that forced his eyes open. Teresa was standing between him and the wall, naked, looking up at him. "Stone told me about James. Yes, he was a part of it, but I swear to you, I had no idea he was Kelly's husband."

"Did he touch you?" he grumbled in a very hard voice.

A tear fell on her cheek. "Yes," she whispered. "He was one of the men who raped me."

Tate's arms came off the wall and wrapped around her tiny body, pulling her to his chest. "I'm so sorry."

"It's not your fault. I just didn't know who he was. I didn't know who any of them were except for Sully and Ted." She sobbed.

Tate reached around to lift her face to his. "I'm sorry," he whispered against her mouth as he brushed his lips across hers.

She moved her hands up his back, around to his chest, and up over his shoulders. Tate lifted her as she wrapped her legs around his waist. The second he felt the warmth of her center on his stomach, he was instantly hard.

"I need you," she whispered into his mouth. "I need you to make me feel. I need you to make me feel whole."

Tate deepened the kiss, his hands moving from her back to her ass. Each of his hands fit over each cheek. His long fingers brushed against her lips, causing her to tense and moan.

It was Teresa who moved, pulling herself up and slowly moving down. If Tate's eyes weren't closed, he would have rolled them to the back of his head. She felt fantastic wrapped around his cock. He tried very hard to restrain himself. He wanted nothing more than to fuck her within an inch of her life.

"Oh God, Tate," she mumbled as she moved. He was letting her do this at her own pace.

"I know, beautiful. Believe me, I know," he growled.

"Ahh," she moaned. "You feel so deep." She panted.

"You feel so incredible, like silk around me," he groaned in her ear.

Tate grabbed her face and seared her with a kiss. When he pulled away, he began his slow and tortuous pace. Growing with intensity and speed as he continued, their grunts and moans become more intense.

He slipped his hand to where they were joined and found her swollen nub. "You need to let go, beautiful," he whispered into her neck as he flicked her.

Her whole body responded to his touch, to his cock buried deep inside her. "Oh God, Tate, I'm going to come," she cried out.

He quickened his pace. "Let it go, beautiful. Let it go and take me with you." He felt her contract around him, squeezing his cock and cradling it in her silken center. "That's it, beautiful," he rasped as she came undone. Two more thrusts and she was over the edge, her body covering with goose flesh as she pulsed around him. "Oh fuck," he called out as he climaxed with her, pouring all of his heat deep inside her.

Teresa's hands slipped off the wall, and Tate pulled her against his heaving chest. He could still feel her pulsing around him, her hips moving in a gentle rocking motion, milking him. He kissed her neck and the side of her face while she calmed down. Her hands entwined in his as he held her. They sat there on the floor of the shower.

When she stopped pulsing, Teresa moved off of Tate and turned, climbing back on his lap and putting her hands on his face. She kissed him. "Please, believe me that I am not going to do anything to hurt you."

Tate didn't say anything, he just kissed her. "I'm sorry I hurt you," he whispered.

She shook her head. "No, I am the one hurting you. As you uncover each piece of information, I look even guiltier of withholding things from you. But I'm not. I just don't know what is important." Tears rolled down her cheeks. "Tate, I am going to be honest with you." She paused and lowered her voice to a near whisper. "I have never felt this way before. No man has ever made me feel like you do."

He smiled. "I'm sure you've just forgotten what it's like. It couldn't have been easy for you with him."

She was shaking her head. "I never once had an orgasm in a man's mouth. With you, all you had to do was touch me."

"I know, beautiful. All I want to do is touch you. But we can't do this. We need to stay sharp. We are gone in less than twenty-four hours. I really wish you would stay here so I can focus."

"Please, don't make me stay. I need to be there when he is ended. I need to watch him die."

Tate wrapped his arms around her. "I know."

They got out of the shower and dressed, then moved upstairs to eat and finalize their departure.

"You two get everything straightened out?" Stone asked without looking up from his computer.

Tate laughed. "Not really. But we have come to an understanding."

Teresa continued to the table to get some food. She sat next to Jones.

"When you're finished, I'd like to check you over," he told her. "I've got some liquid antibiotics and think you could use a shot. We need to keep the healing of those wounds on your back going. I'd hate to go through all this shit and have you die of an infection when it's done."

Teresa smiled. "That'll be fine."

Tate sat with Stone and worked out their plans for departure and for when they arrived back in Chicago. Teresa went in the bedroom with Jones.

"I'm going to need you to remove your shirt so I can check on those lash marks across your back."

Teresa nodded and sat on the bed facing away from Jones. Lifting her shirt up, she covered her chest while Jones put some salve on her marks. "These are healing up very nicely."

"Yeah, Doc had some good salve."

Jones chuckled. "We all use the same thing," he said as he finished up. "For tonight, I want you to wrap your body so it can sink it. We probably aren't going to have another chance to do this. I'll bring the antibiotics with me, so we can get those in you once a day at least. Here." He laid a wrap on the bed. "We use these in the field when someone gets hurt."

"Thank you," she whispered.

"Okay, now, I'm going to need one of your cheeks."

Teresa pulled down her sweats, exposing her right ass cheek. Jones swabbed it and gave her a shot. She pulled them up as he was packing up his bag. "I'll send Tate in so he can help wrap you."

She nodded and he left. Sitting there on the bed, she began to shake. This was all going to happen and soon. They hadn't filled her in on anything, so that meant they didn't trust her. Shaking her head, she fought the tears welling in her eyes. There was a soft knock on the door and then it opened.

"Hey, beautiful, Jones said you needed some help."

She nodded and picked up the bandage roll. "He said I need to wrap this around me tonight so the salve penetrates the wounds. But I can't get it on by myself, and well…" She stopped talking.

"Not a problem. You all right?" he asked, concerned.

"Not really. I'm scared of what's to come." She lifted her arms in the air while Tate began to wrap her. "I've never been this sort of woman, the kind that cries all the time. I've never been afraid of anything. Now, I am afraid of the damn dark. I'm afraid to be alone. When I hear a door slam, I go into full on panic mode."

Tate secured the bandage. "It's understandable with what's happened to you. But, Teresa, you survived. God only knows how, but you did. If you weren't that strong woman, you would have never gotten out of there alive."

She wiped her tears. "But I'm not her anymore."

"Turn around," he whispered. She turned to face him. "You are her. I don't know anyone that would fight me the way you have."

She chuckled. "I was so mad."

He put his finger on her chin, lifting her face to his. "You should be mad. Pissed as a mad hatter at what he did to you. Beautiful, no man should take from a woman like that." Her lip quivered. He couldn't stop himself; he wiped her tears with his thumbs and kissed her. She kissed him back in desperation. Pulling back, he said, "You should get some rest. You may not get the chance to get undisturbed sleep for a while."

Nodding, she put her shirt back on as Tate got off the bed, pulling the covers back. "Will you stay with me?" It was a whisper he wasn't sure he heard, so he didn't answer. Teresa climbed under the covers, and Tate tucked her in. As he was standing to leave, she touched his hand. Looking down, he could see the want in her eyes.

Bending to kiss her, he whispered, "I'll be in later." She smiled and nodded as his lips gently brushed against hers.

CHAPTER TEN

Tate left Teresa to get some rest while he and the guys finalized the exit plans from the island.

"She all right?" Stone asked.

"Yeah, Jones needed her wrapped."

"Listen, man, you are my friend, and I'm here because you called me, because you needed my help. So, you need to tell me what is going on."

Tate looked at him and went to the kitchen to grab a bottle of Jack and two glasses. Sitting down, he poured a drink in both. He drank his down in one gulp and poured another. "That's just it, I don't have a fucking clue. When I found her on the road, I was terrified when I picked her up. It was Jenny all over again. I felt something I wasn't sure I was ever capable of feeling. When that bastard took my mother and I thought I ended him, my heart went cold. But for some reason, it seems to be beating again."

Stone chuckled. "Yeah, I know what you mean."

Tate looked at him. "Don't tell me you…" He paused.

"Listen, man, I am going to tell you something. Something I have kept to myself for the better part of five years. It's Kelly."

Tate sat there looking at him. "I kind of figured as much."

"Well, why didn't you say something?"

"I figured you were an honorable guy and you wouldn't have acted on it either way. She was just married."

"Yeah and look how that shit turned out. Fuck, she is going to be devastated when she learns her husband is in Sully's pocket." Stone shook his head.

Tate leaned in. "When this is said and done, she is going to need someone. I wouldn't have a problem with that. I know you would never hurt her."

Stone looked at him. "What about Teresa?"

"See, that's just it. She's been through a serious, traumatic experience, and it's going to get worse. I think what we are doing is some sort of comfort for her. I mean, I fucking rescued her, so I'm sure what she's feeling is some sort of connection. I don't know, man, but I can't seem to keep my hands off her." He shook his head. "She's like a drug. Once I had a taste, it's all I've wanted."

Stone laughed. "I never had a taste of Kelly, and for five years, I have been in the same place you are. Don't get pissed at me, but I've been keeping an eye on her all this time."

"Yeah, I know. Manny found out a few years back. Made me feel good to think you were watching my back. Of course, I didn't know you were secretly pining away for her." He chuckled, finishing his glass. "Listen, I'm going to get some shut eye. We're up in ten hours. Try not to disturb me." He smiled.

"You should try to sleep some of that time. I'll have the guys stay away."

Tate nodded and got up. "For what's it worth, it would be an honor to have you with my sister. She couldn't do better."

"Thanks, man."

Tate smiled and went back to his room. Teresa was curled around a pillow in the center of the bed. She looked so small. If he didn't know she was there, he could've missed her. Tate dropped his clothes, except for his boxers, and climbed into bed, taking the pillow from her. Her eyes opened slowly and met his. Tate watched as her pupils dilated and lust filled her eyes. He smiled sweetly at her, his cock getting harder as the seconds ticked by. He hadn't felt like this in a very long time, when a smile could get him hard. Her tiny hand came up and touched his face. She moved her body into his and gently kissed him.

He felt her hand move to his chest, and she pressed on him, pushing him back slightly. Tate rolled onto his back as she pulled her body on top of him, him wrapping his arms around her, and they lay like this kissing for a few minutes. God, she tasted so good; he could've kissed her all night long.

She pulled back and whispered, "Can I look at you?"

Tate moaned and nodded his head. Smiling, Teresa reached to turn on the small light next to the bed, casting a yellow hue on his body. Sitting up, she straddled him, sitting on his stomach. If she moved back a few inches, she would feel his rock-hard cock. "Close your eyes and feel," she whispered, planting a small kiss on his lips.

Tate closed his eyes as she moved her tiny hands across his shoulders then down to his chest. She pinched his nipples between her fingertips, and his cock jumped. He felt her move, and then her warm mouth suckled first one nipple and then the other. Shimmying down lower to touch his stomach, she pushed his cock against her ass, and his hands came up and grabbed her hips. Gently, she removed them, whispering, "No touching." Tate smiled, and she continued her exploration of his body.

He felt her climb off of him and position herself between his legs. She ran her fingers along the waistband of his boxers, then along the outline of his cock straining against the cotton material. "You're so hard," she whispered as she stroked him with both hands. She reached for his balls through the material. Squeezing gently caused his hips to raise, pushing his covered cock up into her hands. It was an involuntary action. He was so into the electric feeling her hands were causing. She slowly moved her hands up the length of him to the waistband of his boxers and then slipped her fingers inside and pulled down, releasing him. He lifted his ass so she could get them all the way off.

Having settled back into her place, she sat there looking at him. "You are so beautiful," she whispered. His body was sculpted, rippled with muscles. Every one of them were tight in anticipation of what she was going to do. She placed her hands on his thighs and slowly, gently inched her way up, pushing his legs farther apart until he was spread wide for her viewing pleasure.

His balls hung between his legs, and as she reached to cup them, they barely fit in her tiny hand. "Ahhh," Tate moaned as she gently massaged them.

"You are so big, so beautiful. I'm sorry I hurt you here." Her mouth started watering as his cock twitched each time she caressed them.

Tate couldn't speak; he was in a state of pure pleasure. Teresa's hands moved from his balls to place feather-light touches along the length of his cock, all the way to the tip. She felt the pre-cum and wiped it off with her finger. She wanted to taste him, so she brought her fingers to her mouth. Tate had opened his eyes when her hand left him and watched as she slipped her finger in her mouth, closing her eyes to savor him. "Mmm," she moaned.

When she opened her eyes to continue, she locked eyes with Tate and smiled. "You taste musky. Now, close your eyes and enjoy this."

Tate could have blown his load right there just from watching her. She was a fucking siren to him. He would do anything to feel her touch. He was in over his head with her and he knew it. He knew he was going to get hurt. Closing his eyes, he felt her body shift and her hand wrap around the base of his cock. Her breaths feathered the head, and then she gently licked off the rest of the cum.

Slowly, she pulled him into her mouth. To her, he felt like a soft peach. Her tongue licked as her mouth sucked him. She pushed down further, taking him inch by inch until he hit the back of her throat. Her pull back was just as slow, as again and again she took him, each time a bit further.

Tate could feel himself shake; he was going to blow. "Oh God, beautiful," he moaned.

She increased the suction a bit more, and his back arched off the bed. He had never arched his back; no woman had ever made him feel like this. "I'm going to come," he moaned out, as he fought not to. Teresa took him as deep as she could and then swallowed, contracting her throat, and he couldn't hold it any longer. His release was euphoria at its best. He pulsed slowly and forcefully as he spilled himself into her mouth. She gently sucked on him, swallowing every drop of his musky taste. He pulsed and pulsed, until finally, his body relaxed and she continued to gently suckle him. Tate could do nothing but lay there and let her.

When she finished, she kissed her way back up his body, laying herself on him as she found his mouth, kissing him. "Thank you for saving me," she said.

His hands moved up to catch her face as she went to move off of him. He deepened the kiss, making love to her mouth with his tongue. His hands slowly roved down her body, grabbing the edge of her tee shirt. She moaned in his mouth as his fingers grazed her hips, pulling the shirt up. They separated so he could pull it off her head. He gently touched her face, wrapping his arm around her waist as he rolled her over and continued kissing her. He entwined his fingers in hers, bringing her hands above her head and holding them with one of his hands. He straddled her, his cock already hard again, pressing it against her stomach just below her chest.

"Your turn," he whispered. "No touching." He smiled and let go of her hands. His mouth moved down her body at a slow, lingering pace, licking and sucking her taut nipples, listening to her moans and mews. Each breathy sound landed right in his cock. When he reached her sweats, he gently pulled them down, pleased to see she wasn't wearing any panties. When her beautiful red, fluffy mound came into view, he bent to take a deep breath. "You smell incredible," he whispered right before placing a sweet kiss in the center. Moving back off the bed, he removed her pants and dropped them on the floor. Standing there, he now looked at her in the soft, golden hue from the bedside lamp.

She opened her eyes and watched him watching her. With a sly smile on his face, he dropped to his knees and gently, slowly pulled her to the foot of the bed. He placed each foot on the edge of the mattress and spread her legs wide. His hands and fingers touched every visible part of her skin he could reach. Her back arched with his caresses, her hips pressing into the mattress. Tate slid his hands under her ass, gently squeezing it as he lifted her. His thumbs gently pulled at her lips, opening her to him even further. He wanted to see his prize before he wrapped his lips around it.

There it was, her glorious, swollen pink bud. Licking his lips, he looked up at her sprawled out before him. "You are so fucking beautiful," he rasped as he lowered his mouth. His tongue gently brushed against her, and she cried out. He held her still as his tongue brushed along her, his hands on her hips. As he wrapped his warm lips around her clit, he positioned the tip of his tongue underneath that most sensitive spot.

"Ahh," she moaned as her orgasm hit. Tate could feel her body pulse; he could feel her heels push down on the bed. Gently, he suckled her, then just as she was calming down, he gently bit down, sending her pulsing again and again.

While she unraveled before him, he pulled her off the bed and onto his waiting cock, pushing deep into her as she cocooned him in the silken depths of her core. Her body gripped him again and again, nearly sending him over the edge. With his hands under her arms, he lifted her and thrust deep into her, covering her mouth with his to capture her scream. Again and again, Teresa planted her feet on the floor and kept pace with him, until he couldn't hold on anymore.

"Come with me," she moaned in his mouth, and together, they found their release. They held each other, kissing and touching, not talking. Teresa got up, then Tate. When she went to the bathroom to clean up, he climbed on the bed, collapsing onto his stomach with a smile on his face. This was more than just sex. She was becoming his drug of choice. He couldn't get enough of her.

He heard the door open, and he went to roll over but stopped when he felt her hands run up the back of his thighs, touching his balls before she palmed his sculpted ass. Working her way up his back, she outlined each of his scars, kissing them, as he lay on his stomach. When she reached his shoulders, she placed a gentle kiss between them and whispered, "I'm so sorry he did this to you."

"It was a long time ago."

She wrapped her arms around his body, closing her eyes and letting the gentle beat of his heart lull her to sleep. Neither of them moved for a long time. Tate was wrapped in heaven, and finally realized that this was what he wanted for the rest of his life. The only problem was there was no guarantee he would live to enjoy it. When it was all over, she could just walk away. Surely, as an ADA, she couldn't associate with a man who would be wanted for murder. He refused to think of what was to come. Closing his eyes, he just allowed himself to feel the here and now. Tomorrow would be what it would be.

Morning came faster than he had wanted, but none the less, it had come. He woke before Teresa, not wanting to move, but he had no choice. He managed to slide her with him, and she ended up on his chest. He was instantly hard. Looking over at the clock, he realized they had about an hour before everyone started moving about to get everything ready. He trailed his hands up and down her bandaged back, down to her perfect ass.

She stirred at his touch, slowly turning her head up with a sleepy smile on her face. He pulled her body up his so he could kiss her. Just that one kiss was all it took before he was pushing deep inside of her. He wanted to tie her to the bed and fuck the hell out of her, make her scream and beg for more, but he couldn't bring himself to do it. He couldn't help the way her silken center caressed him. He pumped a bit faster and a bit harder, enough to make her perfect tits sway up and down. Moving a bit closer so her nipples would rub against his chest, he fucked her slow and hard. They came hard together, and he collapsed half on her, half on the bed. He repositioned them, pulling her to lay half on him, and kissed her.

A few minutes later, there was a knock on the door. "Give me a minute," Tate called out. Teresa giggled.

"Funny how they waited until we were finished."

"Yeah, you ready for this, beautiful?"

"Yes and no. Listen, no matter what happens, Tate, I want you to know that this, what we have shared here, has meant everything to me. Thank you."

He chuckled. "No need to thank me. It's me who should be thanking you for allowing me to enjoy you and this incredibly beautiful body of yours. It has been nothing but an honor."

She kissed him and climbed off the bed to go to the bathroom, closing the door behind her. Tate heard the shower and got up to put his clothes on. He left her to do what she needed to do, and went out to find Stone having coffee at the table.

"You ready for this shit storm we're about to enter?"

"I'm ready to end this fucker and get my sister out of that fucking safe room."

Stone nodded. "And then what?"

"Then I'm going south. I'm out."

"And Kelly?"

"Well, I thought I would leave that up to you." Tate smiled at him. "Like I said, she couldn't do better than you, man."

Stone nodded. "Then let's get moving. We have a great deal of shit to do before wheels up."

Teresa came out of the bedroom and smiled at Tate. He sat his coffee down, while Stone got up to go start to get ready. Tate stood and wrapped his arms around her. "No matter what happens, this," he motioned between them, "is not over for me. I just need you to know that."

She smiled and buried her face in his chest. Tate kissed her on the top of the head and held her for minute. "We need to get moving."

"What can I do to help?" She pulled back.

"I'm sure Stone can put you to work. He's down two flights and to the left. I have some shit I have to do, so go find him and I will see you later." She went to walk away and Tate grabbed her, kissing her hard. When he released her, she continued on her way.

A few hours later, they all boarded three boats and headed to shore. Once there, they jumped into Jeeps and traveled about fifty miles to an airport, where their group climbed into three helicopters and headed to Chicago. It took about an hour and a half to reach the landing pad in the field outside Arlington.

No one talked; they just moved as one. Climbing into waiting black SUVs with tinted windows, they sped away. Teresa was with Stone in one of the vehicles. He wasn't sure he trusted her enough to let her ride with Tate, and if he was being honest, Tate wasn't all that convinced either. So, together, they decided the least amount of contact between them was the best. Tate needed his head about him, and if Teresa was going to betray them, he would rather Stone take care of her.

They traveled through the streets of downtown past The Black Cat. Stone made note of the five guys from Columbia working the streets around the club. He knew from his intel that three were already on the inside. Sully had no clue who they were, except that they were shopping for his friend, their boss. All was falling into place.

His team in New York had managed to save three more girls and deplete Sully of two more men. That was six guys and nine girls. Sully was pissed, but Alex Welch was even more pissed. He was losing money left and right. No one had been seen or heard, which was how Stone rolled. When they got to base camp, the SUVs pulled into an underground parking garage, and everyone piled out.

They moved as a unit and made their way up to the abandoned floor of the condemned building down the street from The Black Cat. Stone kept Teresa tucked close to his side. She moved with him like she was his shadow. When they entered the floor, he led her to a room with a bed and some food. "You need to stay put for a while. These guys are mercenaries, and if any of them asks, you are mine. Understood? They take what they want. Those girls Sully sells, these guys buy them. When they are done, the girls are gone. Do you understand what I'm saying to you?" He spoke very quietly.

The fear showed in her eyes, and she swallowed hard, nodding that she understood.

"Listen, beautiful girl, do not look at Tate. He knows the drill. If they even suspect you don't belong to me, I will have to kill all of them to stop them from passing you around. I know this is going to sound cold and hard, but you need to become the submissive here. The one

Sully tried to train you to be. Head down, eyes down. When I say jump, you jump, no question. You got that?"

Teresa fought the tears. "Yes, I've got it."

"Good. When it's time to sleep, you will be sleeping with me. I will behave for the most part, but you need to be convincing. Tate knows what must happen here. Please, Teresa, do not make me kill these guys. We need them, and I really would like to survive this. I've got some plans." He reached up and wiped the tears from her cheeks. "That man out there cares very deeply for you, and he is my friend, so you are safest with me."

She nodded and sat on the bed. Stone walked out and shut the door behind him. As he came into the room, one of the mercenaries made a comment about Teresa. "Hey, you bring some fun for us?"

"No, she is mine. She belongs to me. I paid top dollar for her," Stone said, staring the guy in the face.

"No problem. We get our own. She safe."

Stone nodded. "What's going on?"

"Our boss said we follow you. This is what we have; this is what we know. Now, you are the boss. We follow you. But our boss wants to chat with you. You use this phone to call him."

Stone nodded, taking the phone from him and walking back into the bedroom where Teresa was. She sat on the bed, looking at him. He could see she was terrified at the possibility of what could happen to her here. She listened to Stone speak in Spanish for a few minutes then hang up. He knelt on the floor in front of her, putting his hands on her thighs. "I told them you belong to me. Make it look real, beautiful girl." He reached up and put her hair behind her ear as the door opened. Stone reached behind her neck, pulled her face to his, then smiled before he kissed her. Standing, he lifted her, and she wrapped her legs around his waist, deepening the kiss. They were interrupted by someone clearing his throat. Stone pulled back and looked her in the eye. He had a fucking hard on. "What the fuck do you want?" he said without looking to see who it was. Teresa didn't take her eyes off of him.

"Sorry, boss, but we have information," the guy replied.

"I'll be right there," Stone barked.

"Sorry, boss." The guy left and closed the door.

Stone smiled. "What the hell was that, beautiful girl?"

"You told me to play the part. I have already been gang raped, and I'm not about to do it again. At least, not alive."

"Well, that was some play kiss. I am rock fucking hard." He lowered her to the floor. "If I go out there with this," he grabbed his cock, "Tate is liable to break my fucking neck."

Teresa couldn't help but smile. "All I did was kiss you back."

He chuckled, walking to the bathroom attached to the room. He needed to get away from her, to calm the fuck down. What the fuck? There hadn't been a woman to get this reaction from him in years, especially from just one kiss. He finally started to get soft so he made his way back out into the main room. Walking right up to the guy who walked into the room, he looked him in the eyes. "The next time I am in that room with her, and you fucking walk in without an invitation, you will be going back to your boss in a body bag. She is not for your viewing pleasure, and what I do in that room is not for your pleasure. Do you understand me?"

"Sorry, boss."

Stone knew he was checking him out. He knew he was seeing how far he could push him. Stone needed to pull the alpha card. Hopefully, it worked. "What's going on?"

One of the guys had set up a buy of a young girl he saw in the club. Three days, Sully told him, and she was his. The girl turned out to be a sixteen-year-old runaway that one of Sully's goons had picked up on the street. His friend in Columbia was pissed. He was coming up here himself. He had purchased a few girls for his men over the years from Sully, but under-aged girls were unacceptable. As illegal as his dealings were, it never set well with him when it came to young girls being sold into the sex trade.

There was nothing to do but scout and collect intel, so that is what they did. Stone took Teresa with him everywhere they went. If he had to take a piss, she was right there with him. He had to show them that he owned her. When he would bark an order to her, she would comply. She had to sit next to him, on his lap, at his feet, or anywhere he said. She kissed him regularly, and they slept together, naked. But not once did he touch her inappropriately. They faked having sex, so they were heard by the men. All the while, Tate sat back wanting nothing more than to break Sully's neck so he could be with her.

Days went by. They managed to save the sixteen-year-old. They stashed her in one of the abandoned apartments in the building. The men were under orders to not touch the girls they recovered. As the days ticked by, more and more girls were saved and kept safe until they could get Sully. Every conversation, every transaction was being recorded, from every rescue, both in Chicago and New York. So far, the body count was fourteen girls, seven under-aged rescued, and nine guys dead.

They had been holed up at the abandoned building for nine days when a knock came on the door. All guns pointed to the door. Stone went in the bedroom with Teresa and put her behind him with a gun in her hand. "If bullets fly, you get out."

She nodded. One of the mercenaries answered the door. It was Stone's friend from Columbia. His face lit up when he walked in. "Carlos," he said as they embraced.

"My friend, what are you doing in this hole in the wall? Why are you not checked into one of Chicago's finest?" he asked as his eye caught Teresa. "She is the one?" He nodded toward her.

Stone turned. "We're here because his place is down the block, and yes, she is the one."

"She is very beautiful." He turned to look at Tate. "Let's end this." Tate nodded, trying his best not to look at Teresa. "I've made arrange- ments to have a meeting with Mr. Sully on Friday evening, at The Black Cat since that is where we usually meet. I have told him I need six girls, so I will be bringing six men with me. He usually has double that so I can choose. I told him these girls needed to be special. We will meet in his office." He looked at Teresa, knowing she knew where they were meeting. Sully would shackle the girls from the ceiling naked for viewing. She lowered her eyes, fighting the memories. He continued. "You have two days to get everyone in place. This will not be easy."

Stone smiled. "Nothing in this life is easy."

Carlos walked over to Teresa. He put his finger on her chin, lifting her face. "You are very beautiful. A natural redhead?"

Tate fought not to kill the man. He knew what Carlos was thinking.

Teresa nodded her head. Carlos looked at Stone, who shook his head. "Such a shame," he said, looking back to Teresa. "You would have felt things you never knew you could. You do know there is a thin line between pain and pleasure? I am willing to show you that line if you want."

Jones put his hand on Tate's arm to stop him from killing Carlos. Teresa lowered her eyes and said, "No, thank you. I think I've endured enough pain."

Carlos laughed. "I suppose you have. The offer stands, anytime you want." He let go of her face, and Stone put his arm around her protectively.

Carlos turned and looked right at Tate. "Two days and your revenge will be yours."

"I want him alive," Tate growled out.

"You will have him alive." Turning to Stone, he added, "And then we are even, my friend." He put his hand out to shake Stone's.

"We are, indeed, but my door is always open."

"As is mine. Until Friday, gentlemen." He walked out.

When the door shut, Stone looked at Tate and then moved back into the bedroom with Teresa, closing the door behind him. "We need to make this sound real, beautiful girl. You ready?"

She nodded, not knowing what he was going to do. Out of nowhere, Stone slammed her against the door, slapping her in the face, screaming, "Don't you ever disrespect my friends again by back-talking. Who the fuck do you think you are? You belong to me, and you will respect me." He shouldered the door to make it sound like he shoved her again. Grabbing her, he threw her to the floor and opened the door, so the men outside could see her crying while holding her face. "Next time, it will be a beating you will never forget. Now, sit there until I tell you to move." He walked out, leaving the door open.

Terrified to look up, she could feel Tate's eyes on her. She could feel the warmth of his caress as he fought to stay in his spot. Stone looked at him with regret, but Tate knew it had to be done. Teresa knew it had to be done. But none of that made it right. Stone made her sit on the floor for two hours before he came in to go to bed. While he was holding her naked body against his, he said, "I am so sorry for that. I have never hit a woman before. Please, know I did not enjoy that."

Teresa was crying. "I was so scared when he touched me. I thought for sure he was going to take me."

"Do you think Tate would have let him walk out that door with you?" She shook her head. "Trust me, it is killing him not to be in here with you. Two more days and it's over. You can go home to your family. You will be free and they will all be gone."

There was a knock on the door, so Stone slipped on top of her and engulfed her mouth. She wrapped her legs around his waist, and he dry humped her, making it look like they were fucking. The door opened. "Boss, sorry, but we have an emergency." The door closed.

Stone got off her, hard again. "Fuck, I am tired of these tests. Not to mention this fucking hard-on," he mumbled as he got dressed. Teresa burst into tears, wrapping the sheet around her. "Don't cry. It will be over soon." He burst through the door, leaving it open as he went.

"What the fuck did I tell you?" he shouted as he swung at the guy. "No one fucking comes in there when the door is shut."

Teresa looked up and saw Tate standing in her view. His face said it all. He was beyond pissed at seeing her naked in bed with Stone.

"Sorry to interrupt your fuck session, boss, but one of our guys called in. They caught two of Sully's men trying to kidnap three teenaged girls in the park. We didn't know what we should do about it. Do we let them take the girls or do we stop them?"

"My what?"

"Your fuck session with your sub," the guy said.

Out of nowhere, Stone hit the guy so hard he fell to the floor. "My fucking is none of your fucking business. Get the fuck out of here. Now!" Looking at the other guy, he said, "Grab them all. Bring them here." Spinning on his heels, he started back to the bedroom. Tate stepped in his path, looking at him like he was a dead man walking. Stone gave him a look and put his hand on his chest as he passed by. At the door, Stone turned. "Next time, wait until I answer before you open the fucking door." He slammed the bedroom door and looked at Teresa.

"I am so sorry for that," he said as he moved to the bed.

"He saw me, naked in your bed."

"He knows I would never cross that line. I am sorry about the erection, but you are a very beautiful woman and I am after all a man."

"I don't know if I can take much more of this," she said through silent tears.

Stone was finishing getting dressed. "Put your clothes on. I have to go talk to some of Sully's men, and you are going with me. I am not leaving you here."

She nodded and got dressed. Stone turned his back to give her a little privacy. When they were ready, they went into the other room. The guy Stone punched didn't even look up from his computer. "Where are the girls?" Stone asked.

"Two floors up," Someone answered.

"Put the new girls with them. Feed them and give them blankets. How old are these girls?"

"Teenagers, no more than fourteen."

Stone shook his head. "Take the two men down to the basement. We will be waiting for them. The three of you go down and secure the space. Get it ready. Tate, Jones, and Jacobs, you three with me."

The guy who Stone hit asked, "You leaving the bitch here with us?"

Stone walked over and grabbed him by the hair, jerking his head back. "If I won't give her to Carlos, what the fuck makes you think I would give her to you? She is mine. She belongs to me. Question me again," he pulled a knife from his side and pressed it against his neck, "and it will be the last fucking time you speak." He shoved the guy's head down on the table, then released him and walked back to Teresa. "Let's go, beautiful girl." He wrapped his arm around her and pulled her into his side, sheltering her.

They walked down the hall to the stairs. Jacobs and Tate went first, Teresa in the middle, and Stone along with Jones in the back. She was sandwiched between four monstrous men. It was the only chance she had to touch Tate, and her little hand brushed against his arm. Tate closed his eyes as he felt the electricity shoot through his body where her warm hand touched him. He wanted to turn and kiss her hard and deep. But they couldn't. He didn't want to have the knowledge that Stone was sleeping naked next to her, but he did. He trusted his friend; he had no choice.

When they reached the basement, Tate pressed his body against Teresa's, pushing her flat against the wall with Jacobs on one side, Jones on the other. There was no way anyone could see her. She forced herself not to touch him with her hands. But she did lay her head on his back and breathe him in. She could feel Tate relax against her.

Stone walked over to where the two men were sitting tied to chairs, both with black bags over their heads. Looking around, he saw a pipe lying on the floor against the far wall. He nodded his head, and one of the guys went to get it for him.

Stone swung it across one of the guy's knees.

Screaming out, he said, "What the fuck!"

"Oh, you're going to get fucked all right," Stone said into his ear. "What were you doing with those young girls?"

"Fuck you!" he shouted.

"No. Unlike you, I like my women to come to me willingly." He swung the pipe again, slamming it across his thigh. "Now, don't make me ask you again."

In an agonized voice, the guy yelled, "Nothing, I was doing nothing."

Stone moved to the other guy. "You want to tell me?" The guy didn't say anything, so Stone swung the pipe, landing a hit on his knee.

Screaming, the guy answered, "We were supposed to pick them up. They're just little sluts, and we were going to have a party with them."

"They are fourteen years old. Three friends hanging out in the park, and you thought you could just help yourself?"

"You have them; you saw how they were dressed. They wanted it."

Stone was pissed and swung the pipe again, landing on his thigh. Teresa could hear the bone break, and Tate felt her tense. He wanted to reach behind him and touch her to let her know it would be all right, but he didn't dare move.

"You broke my fucking leg," the one cried out.

Stone leaned in. "Well, my friends here are going to break you in. Have a little fun with you. I think turnabout is fair play, don't you? I mean, you took three young girls to play with, and you two are fully grown men. You know what life is about. So, I am going to leave you with my friends who are literally going to tear you new assholes, and when they are done, I'll be back to finish this chat."

He turned, dropping the pipe on the floor, making both men jump. By the time he got to the stairs, the four men watching over them were tearing at their clothes. Stone smiled at Tate and nodded. He moved so Stone could gather up Teresa, who was shaking when he touched her. She was terrified. Tucking her into his side so she couldn't see what was happening, they started up the stairs.

The first guy Stone hit started to scream as he was shoved on the floor on his knees, his clothes cut from his body so he was naked. "No, no, I will tell you all I know! Please! I will tell you," he cried. The big guy behind him had his cock on the guy's ass when Stone turned and put his hand up to stop him. The guy was thrown back in the chair, and Stone, along with Teresa, moved back down the stairs. He kissed her on the forehead, and Tate pressed her against the wall, as Stone walked away.

Tate turned his head toward Jacobs and whispered to her, "I've got you." She reached up to touch his arm, sending electricity through his whole body.

Stone walked over to the naked guy. "So, what's your story?"

"We work for a man named Sully. He owns The Black Cat along with five other clubs."

Stone looked at Tate, thinking they were going to need more men, before turning back to the naked guy. "What were you doing with the girls?"

"We were sent out to round up girls for him."

"I think we've established this already. Why?"

"Sully trains them."

"Trains them?"

"Come on, you can't be that stupid," the guy said.

Stone slammed the pipe across his forearm, cracking the bone. "I know why he wants them. Now, you tell me why."

"Fuck, you broke my arm," he yelled out.

"See, these guys don't care if all your bones are broken. They just want your ass. You better start talking because, if I leave here again, you are on your own."

"He trains them, beats them into submission, then he sells them."

"Have either of you seen this?"

"We all get to participate, especially if they are resistant."

"Where does this take place?"

"In Sully's office in the basement of The Black Cat, but you will never get in there. He has guards everywhere. It's by invitation only."

"Why were you scouting for such young girls? Virginal girls?" Stone wanted to split the guy's head open.

"Sully has a buyer from Columbia coming tomorrow night. The guy asked for young, virgin girls."

"And because you fucks and Sully like to break them in, you have none?"

"No, we have many. They are locked up down the hall from his office. We train them to suck dick. The rest is up to the buyer."

Stone turned to look at Tate and Jacobs. Tate's face said it all. The man was going to combust. He turned back to the naked guy. "Well, you're a virgin in a sense, aren't you? Looks like you're about to find out what it feels like to be beaten into submission while someone five times your size fucks you raw."

"No, no, you said they wouldn't if I talked."

"No, what I said was I would be back to finish the chat. But seeing as how we're done with our chat, I think it's only fair that these guys get something for their efforts, and virgin ass is what they want."

Stone walked to the stairs, and Teresa was tucked into his side. As they moved up them, they could hear the guys screaming as their asses were raped. Teresa felt herself smile. She was pretty sure those two men had raped her as well.

When they reached the bedroom, she turned into Stone's chest and cried. He held her in his arms, trying to comfort her. Usually, he would make love to a woman who was this distraught, and he really wanted to make love to her, but she wasn't his so he just held her.

CHAPTER ELEVEN

Stone pulled back and said, "You need to get it together, beautiful girl. Why don't you lie down for a bit? I need to go talk to the guys. This will all be over tomorrow night. Then you can go home to your family and forget we ever existed." She nodded, and Stone let her go, watching her tiny frame crawl into the bed and disappear under the covers. His heart went out to her. It went out to Tate, knowing that, after tomorrow, they may never see one another again. This time should be between them. Shaking his head, he left the room.

Jacobs came and stood in front of the door to protect her. Stone walked over to the window and looked out. One of Carlos' men spoke up. "The boss has more men here than us. He has sent a message for you." He stood up and walked over to Stone to hand him a piece of paper.

Stone opened the paper. Written inside was the number nine. He looked up at Tate, and then his watch. "We have eighteen hours, then wheels up." Tate nodded, and Stone went to the bedroom, closing the door on his friend. Crawling into the bed with Teresa, he pulled her to him and wrapped his arms around her. "Less than twenty-four hours and it's over."

"I need to end him," she whispered.

"You will, beautiful girl. You will. Now, get some sleep. You need to be alert tomorrow. I am taking it, with your training, you know how to use a gun?"

"Top of my class," she whispered.

"Good, and you will be wearing a vest. I have a Kevlar petite that will fit you. It's reinforced to deflect armor piercing bullets. If you don't take a head shot, you will be fine. You can wear it under your shirt."

She nodded. "Thank you, Stone."

"Hey, there is no need to thank me yet. We still have to survive this." He chuckled. "I know I have an ass beating coming, that I hope I survive."

She lifted her head from his chest. "What do you mean?"

He laughed, "You don't really think he is going to take this lying down, do you?"

"Take what?"

Chuckling, he said, "Seeing you naked in my bed, me walking out there with a raging hard-on? Him knowing you are wrapped in my arms every night. And for this." He leaned in and kissed her. She didn't fight him; she kissed him back. He deserved that and more for doing this, for saving them. Pulling back, he looked at her. "Fuck, you are beautiful, and you taste so sweet." He ran his finger along her jaw.

"But I want him." Tears rolled down her face and landed on his chest.

"And for the first time in years, he is feeling again. He wants you, too."

She nodded and cried herself to sleep in another man's arms—a man who wanted her, who could take her if he chose, but he was a man of honor so she was safe.

A gentle knock woke Stone. "Yeah," he said. Teresa stirred in his arms.

Tate opened the door. "We need to talk," he said. Teresa instantly woke from hearing his voice and rolled over, locking eyes with him. She saw him smile at the realization that she was fully clothed. Stone got out of bed, and they left the room, leaving her alone.

Closing her eyes, she tried to shift through the fear in her mind and find the last time they were together. How gentle he was, the things he said to her, the way he touched her. How it felt to kiss him. She brought her fingers to her mouth and took a deep breath. It was so quiet, too quiet out there. Looking at the window, she could see the light from the early morning through the cracks in the blinds. Gunshots rang through the silence. Two, a pause, and then three more. She was frozen on the bed. Panic rose, and she reached under the mattress and grabbed the gun and clips Stone had put there for her. She silently moved to the door, positioning herself so that if the door was opened she wouldn't be seen.

The door flew open, and Stone ran in the room. When he turned, Teresa was standing ready with the gun pointed at him. "We need to go now." He reached out and grabbed her arm, dragging her behind him as they exited the bedroom. Tate, Jacobs, and Jones were standing in the hall. Together, they moved like one, running down the hall to the stairs. Once in the garage, Tate grabbed her arm and took off running out into the street, leaving Stone and the rest behind in the garage.

They took off in the opposite direction of The Black Cat. Tate didn't talk, he just kept moving. Down one alley and then the next, farther and farther they ran, until he spotted a small rundown hotel and bolted into it. Teresa had her hat on and her hoodie pulled up. The only way to tell she was a woman was from the size of her small body. Tate got a room, and then they disappeared out the side entrance and kept moving. He found a cab and they jumped in, then he gave the guy the address to the train station. Once inside, he purchased tickets to Oklahoma. They made their way to the platform and then disappeared through some security doors into the underground of Chicago.

Traveling the tunnels and pedways, they exited at the Thompson Center on LaSalle Street. Tate hailed another cab, and they went to Grant Park. From there, they made their way down and across Lake Shore Drive to the marina. Tate used a pass key to gain access, and then they made their way, unseen, to a yacht at the end of the last dock.

Once on board and below deck, Tate grabbed her and pushed her against the wall, kissing her. She brought her hands up into his hair and deepened the kiss. It was frantic, as fear fueled them both. Tate pulled away, resting his forehead on hers while they both caught their breath.

Teresa spoke first. "What happened?"

Tate just shook his head. "It's bad. Somehow the F.B.I. caught wind that Carlos is in town. Someone in that room tipped them off, and we know it wasn't one of us. So, we took them out. I took you, and Stone went to talk to Carlos." He covered her mouth again. "I didn't like knowing he was next to you night after night."

Teresa put her hands on his face and kissed him. "He never touched me like that," she whispered through tears.

"Too many times he came out of there with a fucking hard-on," Tate growled.

Teresa pushed on his chest and stripped in front of him. "He never touched me."

Tate stood there looking at her. "You are so fucking beautiful." His hand came up to cradle her face. Her hands moved to take off his clothes. He helped and before they knew what was happening, she was wrapped around him and he was pushing deep inside her. "Fuck, you feel like heaven." He pumped deeper into her.

She hung on to him and took all of his fear, his frustration, his desire, and his passion. Not knowing if they would be alive when this was over, they fucked. They made love, and then they fucked again. As they lay on the floor just inside the door holding one another, Tate swallowed hard. "When this is done, you can go home."

"And what will become of you?" she whispered, kissing his chest.

"Come on, there is a shower on this boat." He got up and gathered up their clothes then led her down a flight of stairs to a cabin. He nodded toward a door. "You go." She didn't say anything as she opened the door and went in. Once Tate heard the water running, he pulled the satellite phone out of his pocket and called Stone. "We're good," he said.

"Yeah, well, the fucking F.B.I. is all over this. Carlos is secure and the deal is still going down. His sources say they have no clue why he is here, just that he is here. He has over a hundred men in this city, so I'm sure word got out somewhere. You two stay put. I'll call you when we're all in position, and you can make your way to the Cat. Soon, my friend, this will be over."

"All right." Tate went to say something else but Stone stopped him.

"Listen, what happened was necessary. You know that, right. I didn't touch her."

"I know, and thanks."

"No thanks necessary, but let me just say this. She is one beautiful woman. You're lucky I love you, man."

Tate chuckled. "Yeah, same here. Otherwise, you'd be dead."

Stone laughed. "See you soon." And he hung up.

Tate put the phone away and went into the bathroom where Teresa was drying off. He moved around her and got in, making it quick. Teresa went to the bedroom and sat wrapped in a towel on the edge of the bed, trying to fight back her tears. She didn't know what was going to become of them. *Was she suffering from Stockholm syndrome? Could she be in love with him after such a short time? Is it just the rush of fear that pushes them together? Is any of this real?* She had spent six months being tortured and raped, fighting the whole time to survive one more day. She shook her head, confused. She was living off the rush of the past.

Tate stood leaning against the wall, watching her struggle with something. He was having the same thoughts she was having. *Could he love her? Would she want him being who she was?* Her DNA couldn't possibly let her love someone like him. He felt so drawn to her, but was it just the best sex of his life, or was it something more? They didn't know much about one another. He didn't even know what her favorite food was. There wasn't any time to discover these things about her. He didn't know if she even wanted him to know. Was she just doing what she thought she needed to do to get the end result, to get Sully?

Teresa reached up and wiped a tear from her cheek. Soon, it would be over and she could go home. She could see her family. She would be safe. Would her apartment still be there? Would her job still be there? Would she even be able to continue with a normal life? What was normal anymore? She willingly put herself in the underbelly of the darkest part of Chicago, and it blew up in her face. She caught Tate out of the corner of her eye and turned her head, wiping her cheeks as she did.

He smiled at her sweetly. "It'll all be over soon," he said softly.

"Then what?" she said.

Tate was shocked at her response; he'd been thinking the same thing. "I don't know, beautiful." He moved to the bed and crawled on behind her. "Come here." He wrapped his arm around her waist. She curled up nearly on top of him. "It will be what it will be."

"Do you know what you want it to be, Tate?"

"I'm afraid to think of anything but the here and now."

She scooted up his body, her towel staying in place but releasing her chest. She kissed him. "Make love to me, Tate. Make love to me like we are going to die tomorrow, like you love me. Let me love you."

She didn't have to ask him twice. *Like you love me*, she'd said, and God help him, he believed in that moment that he did love her. That she was the woman who was put here for just him.

They loved one another for hours, her with her mouth on him and him with his on her. They made slow love, they fucked, and they loved again and again. They laid there sedate, wrapped in each other, eyes closed, hearts beating as one.

When the phone rang, Tate knew it was time, and his body tensed.

"What is that?" she asked.

"That is our signal. Time to go end this, beautiful. Time to get you home to your family."

They got up and dressed. Tate went to the closet and pulled out two vests, handing one to her. "Put it on under your shirt. Its body armor; no one will know you are wearing it."

149

She knew what it was, but she had never seen a vest quite like this one. It fit her perfectly, like a second skin. Together, they moved through the city. Tate checked his watch. Ten minutes and Carlos would be at The Black Cat. They made it a few minutes before he did, positioning themselves across the street in the shadows.

They sat and watched as his black SUVs pulled into the alley. Carlos got out, followed by his men, fifteen in all. Three took up position around the vehicles, two at the door, and the rest went inside with Carlos. Tate checked his watch. Right on time. The minutes ticked by while they waited.

Carlos and his men were escorted to Sully's office, nothing unusual. His men stopped where they routinely did. Sully waited for Carlos at the end of the hallway.

"Mr. Santiago," Sully said.

"Mr. Sully," Carlos acknowledged, walking past him to enter his office. To his left were twenty or more young girls, naked and shackled to the bars hanging down from the ceiling.

As was tradition, Sully came in and closed the door behind him, leaving two of Carlos' men at the door and six of them coming in to stand behind him. Sully poured two glasses of scotch and handed one to Carlos. He took it but did not drink it. He hated the man's cheap liquor. Sully watched as Carlos sat the glass down.

"I see you have what I ordered." Carlos looked Sully in the eye.

"I have that and more."

"The virgins, I would like to see those first," Carlos said, standing.

Sully nodded. "Of course." He held his hand out so Carlos could walk in front of him to the back of the room. "The five here in the front are virgins."

Carlos looked at his men and then walked up to the first girl, and she was a girl not a woman. He touched her skin; it was flawless. It made him sick to his stomach when he looked at her soft pink nipples. These were the nipples of a child. He moved on to the next and the next. None of them could have been older than fifteen years old, gagged and terrified as they hung there naked. "And the conditioned women?" Carlos said to Sully.

"Oh, the rest have been conditioned and shall make wonderful subs." He put his hand out, showing Carlos the rest of the women.

He checked each one out. He saw a redhead and thought of Teresa. Walking up to her, he looked at her face. Not as beautiful, but she would do. He ran his finger down the center of her chest to her mound. Grabbing her pubic hair and tugging, he said to her, "You are not a true redhead?" She shook her head no. He reached up and puckered her nipple in his fingers. "Shall I see how you taste, you false redhead?" He bent and sucked her nipple into his mouth, biting the tip. She cried out. Carlos slapped her in the face. "You will not make a sound."

He turned to one of his men. "Come here, I want to inspect this one." The guy came over. Carlos noticed the young girls crying while a few of the others had lust-filled eyes. "Pick her up and spread her wide." He was going through the motions. This was how he inspected his goods. He needed it to all seem real. The man spread her legs wide, lifting her so Carlos could view her pussy. He touched her, spreading her lips wider, and shoved two fingers deep inside her. She felt a bit loose. "This one here is no good. She is too used up. I like my pussy tight, to grip me better, like the virgins do." He moved on to the next and the next. When he had found two that he liked, he moved back to Sully's desk. "I will take the five virgins and the two in the back," Carlos said, snapping his fingers. One of his men walked up and put a briefcase on the table.

While Carlos was inspecting his goods, Tate and Teresa stood in the shadows, watching as Stone and his crew, along with Carlos's men, invaded The Black Cat. There was no sound; all the guns had silencers on them. Inside, they collected the key players. Eight cops, Ted included, James, and few others who were involved in the kidnapping and transporting of young women. The girls and women were herded out into a waiting van. In New York, the same thing was taking place. When the phone in Tate's pocket rang, he looked at Teresa. Together, hand in hand, they walked out of the shadows and across the street to the back of The Black Cat. Stone met them at the door, and they went to stand outside of Sully's office.

~

Sully smiled at Carlos. "It was good doing business with you, Mr. Santiago." He reached out to shake Carlos's hand.

"Aren't you going to count it, make sure I didn't short change you?" Carlos said with a small grin. He knew this scumbag was done. He wanted to see his face when he opened the case.

"I trust you, Mr. Santiago. We've done business before."

Carlos stood up and moved to the door. "Yes, Mr. Sully, but we will never be doing business again." Carlos turned as six guns all pointed at Sully's head, their triggers cocked.

Sully looked at him. "You do realize that you will never get out of here alive." His tone was very arrogant, and he laughed.

"Ah, but you see, Mr. Sully, that is where you are mistaken. It is you who will not leave here alive." He opened the door, and Stone walked in first, followed by ten of his men. Carlos left. Passing Teresa in the hall, he took her hand, placing in it a card. "If you ever need anything," he whispered in her ear as he walked away.

The men worked silently, releasing the girls and women, herding them out to the waiting van. Two of Carlos's men dragged Sully over to the racks and handcuffed him to them.

"What the fuck are you doing?" he screamed. Stone punched him in the face and knocked him out. Jacobs and Jones dragged in James, Ted, and the other cops, hanging them in place. All of them were unconscious.

Stone left to thank Carlos and his men. "Whatever you need, my friend," Carlos told him. They shook hands and Stone watched as he drove away.

Making his way back downstairs, he ran into Tate and Teresa. "From the way I see it, you have about fifteen minutes. We will wait out here."

Teresa nodded then turned to walk in the room where she'd been raped and tortured for six months. Stone put a club in her hand. "Get it all out, beautiful girl. Become whole again."

With her head held high and Tate behind her, she went to end this. Walking in the room, she found it hard to breathe. There he was, there they all were. Each of these men hanging here had raped her, had tortured her, had shoved their cocks in her mouth, in her ass, and the whole time laughed about it. They had taken sadistic pleasure in her body against her will.

She couldn't stop the anger. Walking up to Sully, she swung the club, hitting him in the knee, and listened as it shattered. His eyes popped open with a gut-wrenching scream, which was cut short as he realized who'd hit him. "You fucking little cunt, I will kill you!" he screamed at her. She pulled a knife out of her pants and walked behind him. She slit his clothing off, letting it fall to the floor.

"You first," she whispered in his ear as she pushed the knife into his lower back. Tate stood with his arms crossed, watching her take her revenge.

"Fucking whore," he said.

Tate moved in front of him. "Hello, Father," he said.

Sully shut up and looked at him. "I was never your father, you little fuck. You're a piece of shit, just like your stupid fucking mother." Tate slammed his fist into Sully's stomach, then punched him in the face, knocking him out.

Teresa had moved to Ted, swinging her club across his knees, shattering them. He screamed out, opening his eyes. "Hello, my love," she said to him.

"What the fuck?" he gasped.

Tate moved behind her. "I'm sorry to disappoint you, darling, but your career as a cop is over," she cooed at him.

"Fuck you! You can't touch me."

She laughed. "Oh, darling, we are not stupid. The F.B.I. is here. We know how far and how deep this goes. But your life will end here."

"Fuck you! You are nothing but a used up little whore." She slowly pushed her knife into his chest, puncturing his lung.

"That may be so, but I am going to have the pleasure of watching you drown in your own blood." She got up on her tippy toes and kissed him on the mouth. "See you in hell," she said as she plunged the knife in again.

Next, she moved to James, swinging her club, shattering his knee caps. He opened his eyes, screaming, but his cries were cut off when Tate grabbed him by the throat. "Hello, brother-in-law. Surprised to see me?"

James struggled to talk, so Tate let him go. "Oh my God, Sully blackmailed me. You have to help me, Tate. He has Kelly and Taylor hidden somewhere."

Tate moved, and Teresa was there. "Does he now?"

James looked from Tate to Teresa. "You cannot believe this bitch. She is fucking crazy."

Teresa smiled at him and pushed her knife in, just under his ribs, slicing his liver. "You will never get the chance to hurt another woman again." She pulled up on the knife while he screamed.

They continued around the room, doing this to each of the men. All of them were hanging there bleeding to death.

Sully started to come around. "Fucking little bitch," he muttered. Teresa and Tate walked up to him.

"I saved you for last." Teresa dragged her knife across his chest, flaying him. "You will not see the light of day again. I told you that I would come for you. I told you that, if you let me live, you would die. You didn't listen to me, and now here you are."

"I'm still alive, bitch," he groaned. Then, looking at Tate, he said, "You were nothing but a fucking pussy as a kid, and you are still a pussy letting a woman dictate you."

Tate laughed. "I got my revenge already. This isn't mine, but I sure am enjoying it. You made the mistake of coming after me. I didn't know you were alive, but the minute I did, you knew you were marked for death."

"Ha," he said as Teresa came around to face him.

"You look scared, Sully, really scared," she taunted.

"Fuck you, bitch." He spat in her face.

She grabbed his cock. "With this? I don't think so." She pulled it away from his body and dragged her knife across it, cutting it off. Sully screamed, and she shoved it in his mouth as far as it would go, shutting him up. She smiled. "How does it feel to have your cock shoved down your throat? Not fun, is it?" He was gagging and choking trying to scream from the pain.

She turned to Tate. "I'm done now."

Tate reached down and took her knife as she passed by him heading for the door. He looked Sully in the face, slamming the knife in his gut just above his hairline and dragging it up his chest, gutting him. He died with his dick in his mouth, hanging by chains he had bound her with. They walked out together. Stone watched them as they made their way up the stairs.

Stone walked in and looked at the insane scene they left. Eleven men, dead, each with a different knife wound. He smiled, shook his head, and dropped a huge file folder on Sully's desk. It contained all the information they had gathered.

Once everyone was out of the building, Tate, Teresa, Jacobs, Jones, and Stone stood in the alley by the truck that housed all the girls. Teresa seemed to be in shock just standing there, so Tate began to remove her clothes. She didn't fight him; she just stood there with her fists clutched in tight balls. When he finished, she stood there in her bra and panties.

Jacobs put her clothes in a plastic bag and put them in the SUV. Tate put his hands on her face. "It's done, beautiful. It's over and you are free now. Go home to your family. They will be waiting for you." She blinked back the tears as he kissed her goodbye.

Jones opened the back of the truck, and Tate lifted Teresa into the compartment with the rest of the girls. He watched her watching him as they closed the door.

Stone was on the phone in the background, talking to the F.B.I., giving them a tip. He hung up and called his guys to let Teresa's family go home, then walked up to Tate. "Let's go get Kelly." He nodded and walked to the SUV, and they could already hear approaching sirens as they drove off. It took about an hour and a half to get to the house.

While they drove to Arlington, the F.B.I. had showed up at The Black Cat. All the men were dead, and when they opened the doors to the truck, they found fifty women, twelve teenaged girls that had been kidnapped, and Teresa. No one knew who she was because she had been missing for so long. She was going to be taken to the hospital along with the rest of the girls. She was still in a state of shock.

Tate and Stone made it to the house. Tate cleaned out the safe and then tripped the release to the panic room. Kelly and Taylor were sleeping.

"Hey, baby girl," Tate said to Kelly as he moved her hair off her face.

Her eyes fluttered open. "Tate?" she whispered.

"Yeah, it's me."

Kelly jumped up and threw herself into his arms, crying. "Oh God, I was so scared. I didn't know what I was going to do. Is it over? Are we safe?"

Tate held her close. "It's over. It's over and he's dead." She sobbed in his arms while he held her. "Come on, let's get out of here. We need to keep moving." She nodded, pulling back to gather up Taylor. "I'll get her. You go with Stone."

Tate picked up Taylor and snuggled her into his chest, and they all left. When Kelly got in the SUV, Tate placed Taylor in her lap and buckled them both in. He climbed in the other side, and Stone drove off. When they reached the gate, Stone stopped and Tate turned around. He pressed a button on a remote trigger and watched his house blow up, and the four of them disappeared.

CHAPTER TWELVE

Teresa sat in the back of the truck staring into space with tears streaming down her cheeks. He'd left her. He'd left her here all alone. The girls were crying out loud and talking, and some were banging on the truck. It went on for what seemed like hours to Teresa. Why would he leave her like that? He said it was real for him.

Suddenly, the door to the truck flew open and it was flooded with light. There were F.B.I. agents everywhere. The girls were screaming and crying, telling anyone who would listen what had happened to them. All the while, Teresa just sat there, clutching her only thread of the truth in her hand. What was she supposed to do? Was she supposed to tell them she killed those men? Was she supposed to wait for him to come and get her? She felt hands on her; they were warm hands, gentle hands, kind hands. She looked up into the blank face of the person touching her. It wasn't him. He helped her kill Sully and then he left her.

The hands wrapped a blanket around her and held her close. She pushed the hands away and cowered inward, away from the people who were meant to help her. She didn't want anyone to help her. She wanted him. She wanted him to hold her, to comfort her. But he'd left.

CIN MEDLEY

A woman walked up to her. "Hi, I'm Sherry. Do you want to come with me so we can get you checked out?"

Teresa looked at her and nodded. Sherry gently guided her to an ambulance, then helped her up into it. A man touched her, and she flinched away from him. "It's all right, my name is John. I'm an EMT. Can I look you over?" She cowered away from him, hiding her face in the blanket. She didn't want anyone to touch her. She only wanted Tate, but he left her there. John climbed out of the ambulance and went to get two women to help her. "She won't let me touch her, not that I blame her," he explained to them.

Teresa stood in the ambulance crying, wanting nothing more than to be with Tate. She heard a woman talking to her. "Hi, I'm Sue, and this is Mary." Teresa turned her head to look at them, then she looked around for John. Mary turned to shut the doors. "Can we look you over, make sure you are all right?" Teresa nodded as she guided her to sit down. "Would it be all right if I took your blanket off?" She let it go and sat completely still while they checked her over. "I'm going to put an IV in your arm so you can get some fluids. Okay?" She held out her arm, but Sue couldn't get a vein. "Okay, how about we take you to the hospital. We will go with you. Can you tell me your name?"

Teresa just sat there. She picked up her blanket and pulled it tighter around her, clutching the only piece of reality she had. She heard Sue talking to the driver, but she had no idea what she said. The ambulance started moving, but her mind was still in the alley kissing Tate. She closed her eyes, trying to sear the memory in her mind. Tears fell freely down her cheeks.

Time passed with no meaning, when she realized that things had changed. A police woman was standing next to her bed, touching her arm. Teresa looked at her as she was talking, but she didn't hear anything she said. She just stared at her. She looked around the room. There was a nurse on one side of her, and another policeman by the door.

"What?" she whispered. "What do you want? Please, just leave me alone."

"Do you know who you are?" the woman asked gently.

"Yes, how long have I been here?" she whispered, afraid to speak any louder.

"Four days. There are just a few of you left in the hospital."

"A few of who?"

"Girls from the truck. We've pieced together most of what happened. Now, we are trying to find your family. Can you tell me your name?"

Teresa closed her eyes, trying to fight back the tears. But they fell anyway. "My name is Teresa Barns," she whispered and rolled away from the police woman.

That name sounded familiar to her, then it hit her. "Are you Teresa Barns, the Assistant District Attorney?" She nodded. "Oh my God," the woman whispered. "Oh my God. Do you want me to contact your family?"

"Please, just leave me alone." Teresa sobbed. The nurse and the policemen left. She laid there in the darkness for hours, crying, thinking about where he was. Why wasn't he there with her? There was nothing but the card in her hand. She opened her hand and looked at the phone number and the initials C. R. S. on it. This was her truth that all she endured was real. He was real. She closed her hand around the card and then closed her eyes.

She woke to a murmur in her room. Deep voices trying to sound soft. Her eyes shot open. Was it him? She slowly rolled over to see her family looking at her. Some of them were crying, some were smiling. Her mother went to move, but her father put his hand gently on her arm. She searched the room, but he wasn't there. He wasn't coming for her. He had left her alone. She closed her eyes and rolled back over, trying to stop her tears. She could hear her mother sobbing. "Please, just leave me alone," she said. Her sister touched her arm, and Teresa cowered away from her. One by one, they left her room. One by one, the tears fell. Piece by piece, her heart broke. Why had he left her?

In the hallway, her parents were speaking to the doctor. "She has been through a horrendous ordeal. Her injuries are horrific to even me, and I've seen a lot. Her ovaries have been removed. Her arms, legs, jaw, nose, and fingers have been broken and healed numerous times. She has eighteen whip lashes on her back, and a few reached around to her stomach. She has numerous scars, but from what, we don't know. She hasn't spoken at all. She just stares off into space and cries. She is clutching a card in her hand. We tried to take it from her, but she just squeezes hard. She has been tortured beyond belief."

Teresa's mother tried to steady her voice. "Was she raped?"

The doctor nodded his head. "She suffered the worst of these girls."

"Yes, we heard the story on the news, some sex trade business. It was the man she was trying to prosecute. And her boyfriend was the one who helped them get her. They were all found dead. But what about Teresa?" her father asked.

"We don't know anything. Some of the girls remembered her, but she was kept away from everyone. We don't know anything. She isn't talking," the doctor restated.

"Maybe her sister can talk to her. She was always closer to her," Teresa's mother suggested.

"We are going to suggest to her that she see someone professionally. Maybe that will help her," the doctor suggested.

"No, she won't do that. She is a very independent person. Let us see if we can help her. When can she come home?"

"Well, I'd like to keep her for a few more days, get some more fluids in her and some more antibiotics. So maybe two days."

"Thank you, Doctor."

He nodded and walked away. Teresa's parents stood just outside her door looking at one another, feeling helpless. How do you help someone you love who has endured such torture? Her mother turned and walked to her door. Pushing it open, she went in alone. She walked over to the bed and gently moved the hair from her face. Teresa flinched and cowered away from her. With tears falling on her cheeks, her mother bent and kissed her head, whispering, "I love you." Then she left her daughter to cry herself to sleep again.

Two days passed, and she still ate nothing, said nothing. The doctor and her sister came in. "Good morning, Teresa," he said. "Your

sister has come to take you home today. You ready to go?" She just
stared at the wall behind him. She didn't care where she went. She just
wanted to be alone with her memories of their time together. Her
sister, Vickie, helped her get dressed, smiling here and there. She
reluctantly got in the wheelchair.

"Sweetie, the press is out front, so be prepared. Hospital security is
going to help us get to the car," her sister said.

Teresa nodded and prepared herself for the onslaught of flashes
going off and people screaming at her. As they walked out of the
hospital, people gathered around them.

"Ms. Barns, who rescued you?"

"What did they do to you?"

"How long were you captive?"

"Are the stories true that you were tortured?"

She closed her eyes as her sister fought their way through the
crowd. The car was parked right at the entrance. Security helped her
get in the car, and her sister drove away as fast as she could. "I am so
sorry about that," Vickie said to her. Teresa kept her eyes closed as
more tears fell. Vickie reached out and took her hand. Teresa pulled it
away, brought her knees up to her chin, and stared out the window.

When they got to Vickie's apartment, Teresa found a chair and
turned it toward the window, where curled up in it, not saying a
word.

"I got some of your clothes from Mom and Dad's. I put it all in the
spare room. I went and picked up some of your favorite foods. All
your shower stuff is in the bathroom in your room, so you are all set.
Can I get you anything?"

"Do you have any scotch?" Teresa said in a soft voice.

"No, but I can go get some. I'll be right back," Vickie said as she
grabbed her purse off the table and then left.

Teresa sat there with her eyes closed, thinking about him. She
wondered what he was doing now, where he was. Still clutching her
card, she opened her hand to look at it. The number was starting to
fade. She got up and went to the room that would become hers.
Looking around, she saw a few of her things. Her jewelry box was on

the dresser. She walked over to it and pulled the drawer out, then went in the kitchen and found some tape, and she taped the card to the back of the drawer and pushed it back in. It was her only thread to him.

Her sister returned to find Teresa standing at the dresser, looking at her hands. "I got the scotch. You want to have a drink?"

Teresa nodded and walked behind her sister to the kitchen. When Vickie poured the amber liquid into a glass and handed it to her, she drank it in one gulp. Setting her glass down, she motioned for Vickie to pour more. She did. Again, Teresa drank it down, and again, Vickie poured more. She did this five times. The sixth glass she took with her and went to sit in the chair. Vickie followed her.

"I know you don't want to, or can't, talk about what happened to you, and that's all right. I just want you to know that I am here. I've missed you so much. We looked and looked for you. Hell, we were looking for you the day those men came and took us away. Why did they do that? No one said a word to us."

"To protect you," Teresa whispered.

"Did you know they did it?"

"Not for about a week."

"Sweetie, who were those men?"

"Friends of friends," she said as tears rolled down her cheeks.

"Sweetie, what is going on in your head?"

Teresa just shook her head. She couldn't talk about it. Hell, she couldn't even think about it without crying. It was over, and just like he promised, she was home safe with her family.

"I am safe. I am home just like he promised," she whispered through her tears.

Vickie sat looking at her sister, feeling her own tears coming. "Who, sweetie? Who promised?"

Teresa drank the rest of her scotch and got up to go into her room, closing the door behind her. She crawled into bed and cried herself to sleep. She didn't want to feel the emptiness that had grown inside her, inside her heart. He had saved her, in every way possible, and then he kept his promise and sent her home.

When morning came, she got up and took a shower. She found some clothes, got dressed, and went out to face her sister. But the only thing she found was a note.

Went to work. See you around 6

Love you

Vickie

Teresa stood in the dining room staring at the note. She got something to eat and then sat in the chair to stare out the window. Hours passed by, and she didn't move. There was a knock on the door, but she didn't answer it. She didn't want to see anyone. Whoever knocked did it again, so she got up and went to her room, closing the door and then crawling into bed. The world outside was a world she wanted no part of.

Days passed by, turning into weeks. Five weeks, then six weeks, and still, she couldn't pull herself out of this funk. Her mother had brought over a huge box full of cards and letters from people who wished her well. Vickie would spend the evenings reading her the cards. Three nights in, she pulled a postcard out. "Hey, here is a postcard." She flipped it over. "It doesn't have a stamp on it. How weird. It says, 'Thinking of you.' That's it." She laid it on the table next to Teresa.

She turned her head to look at the card. It was a picture of a palm tree with the sun shining through it. It didn't mean anything to her, so she looked back out the window. But she couldn't stop her eyes from looking at the postcard. *Thinking of you.* Could it be? Her heart beat faster; in fact, it felt like it had just started beating again. Was this a clue? Was he really thinking of her? She couldn't stop the flood of memories slamming into her mind. For weeks, she worked to put them away, trying to get back to her life, but they were never far from the front of her mind.

"I think I might go for a walk," Teresa said. She got up and put on her shoes. Her sister was freaking out. For weeks, she hadn't left the house. She hadn't said much either. But now, she wanted to go for a walk, at ten at night.

"Do you want me to come with you?" Vickie asked.

"No, I'll be fine," she said as she put her hood up and tucked her hair into it. Vickie watched as she walked out the door.

Picking up the phone she called their mother. "Mom, she just got up and walked out the door. What do I do?"

"Did she say anything?"

"She said she wanted to go for a walk."

"Well, then she went for a walk. Honey, you need to just be there for her. She will start to come back on her own. She went through something horrible, and her mind needs to recover."

"Mom, I don't think that's it at all. I think there is something more going on. I asked her if she knew who the men were who came and took us away. She said they were friends of friends. Then I asked her if she knew we were there, and she said not for a week. Mom, I think she was somewhere else when we were taken. She wasn't with that man that hurt her. Mom, something more is going on."

"Vickie, she is probably confused. Just let her be. Call me when she gets home so I don't worry. I love you, honey."

"Love you, too, Mom." She hung up. When she laid the phone down, the postcard caught her attention. She picked it up and looked at it. This card was put in their mailbox by hand. There was no postmark on it. "Who sent you?" she asked the card.

Vickie put the card in Teresa's room on her dresser. If it meant something to her, maybe it would spark something in her mind. Too many weeks had passed. She didn't believe her sister was withdrawn because of what she lived through. If she had already been rescued the day they were taken, she had been with someone, somewhere, for weeks before she was found in that truck. Vickie looked around Teresa's room. She had that paper clutched in her hand the whole time she was in the hospital and then for days here. Wondering where it went, Vickie looked in her drawers. She looked in her jewelry box next, and as she pulled out the drawer, she heard what sounded like scraping. She pulled the drawer out all the way. Taped to the back was the card. Careful not to tear it, she gently peeled it off.

The only thing on it was a number and the initials C. R. S., so she wrote the number down and replaced the card, slowly pushing the drawer back. She left her sister's room and went into her own. She turned on her laptop and tried to search the number. Who was C.R.S.? Was this the person who rescued her, who kept us safe, who kept her safe? For over an hour, she couldn't figure out the number. She had a friend at work who could manipulate a computer like the best of them. Tomorrow, she would give the number to him, see if he could figure it out. Vickie heard the door shut, so she closed her laptop and went out in the living room.

"Did you have a nice walk?" she asked.

"I got some rocky road ice cream. You want some?" Teresa said.

Vickie just stood there, surprised. "Sure."

They sat in the chairs facing the window, eating ice cream. When she finished, Teresa got up. "I am going to take a shower and go to bed." She headed for the kitchen to put her bowl in the sink. "Vic, thanks for letting me stay with you," she said and continued into her room. Closing the door, she found herself staring at the postcard. With shaking hands, she picked it up and turned it over. Her fingers ran across the writing. She didn't know what his writing looked like; she didn't know if this was from him or if it was a trick. She smiled, turned the card over, and went to take a shower. After, as she laid in bed, she thought of him.

Vickie smiled. Was her sister finally coming back? Did it have something to do with that postcard? She heard the shower turn on, and she shut off the lights to go to bed.

CHAPTER THIRTEEN

Vickie woke earlier than usual. She wanted to get to work to talk to Sam about the number. She jumped in the shower and headed out. Teresa was still in her room when she left. By the time she got to work, Sam was just coming in behind her.

"Sam, hi, I was wondering if you could do something for me."

He smiled at her. "I can and will do whatever you need. What's up?"

They walked to his workstation. "Well, I found this number. I think it's a phone number, but I can't seem to track it down. I was wondering if you could tell me where it is and who it belongs to."

"Sure, it shouldn't take too long. Give me the number and I will get right on it."

Vickie wrote the number down and then went to her office. She tried to concentrate but couldn't; her mind was too distracted by wanting to know. There was a knock on her door. "Come in," she called out.

Sam came in and closed the door behind him. When he turned around, Vickie got nervous. "What's the matter Sam?"

He swallowed and sat down. "Where did you get this number?"

"I found it written on a card. Why? Whose number, is it?"

His voice got very low. "Vickie, the number is a Columbian number."

She crinkled her brow. "Columbia, as in South America?"

He nodded. She swallowed. "Whose number, is it?"

He sat there looking at her. "Are you sure you want to know?" Vickie nodded, not sure she wanted to know as much as she had to know. "It goes to a satellite phone registered to Carlos Ramirez Santiago."

Vickie looked at him. "Who the hell is that?"

Sam leaned in and whispered, "He is the head of the Columbian drug cartel. He is a very dangerous man, Vickie. Why do you have his number?"

He could have slapped her and she wouldn't have been this shocked. She got up and grabbed her purse. "You need to wipe your computer, Sam. Lose that number and tell no one of this."

"It's already done, but this isn't going to end well. What have you gotten yourself into?"

"It's not me, Sam, but I have to go. I will talk to you later. Thank you." She ran out of her office and made it home in record time. When she opened the door, she froze. There was a very well-dressed man standing in her living room, and Teresa was standing in front of him. She watched as the man touched her sister's face.

"I will do whatever I can to help you. You will owe me nothing. I am jealous of my old friend. You are a rare beauty. I will do my best. Have a good life, Hermosa," he said to her. Leaning in, he kissed her forehead then turned to face Vickie. Smiling at her, he said, "Ah, the sister. Perhaps you should keep your things well hidden, Hermosa. Your sister tried to find me today." He walked by, touching her frozen face. "Lovely, just like your sister," he said to her.

"I'm sorry, it won't happen again," Teresa said softly.

Carlos turned to her, smiling. "Nonsense, I told you, just as I told our mutual friend, whatever you need. You did me a great service, and I will forever be grateful. I hope to see you one day again. Remember, a fine line. I could bring you the greatest pleasure you have ever known."

Teresa smiled at him. "No, thank you. As I said before, I think I've had my fair share of pain."

Carlos nodded and walked out the door.

Vickie stood there staring at her sister. "What the fuck was that?" she said softly.

Teresa smiled at her. "He is a friend."

Vickie came across the room, taking her hand and pulling her into her bedroom. "Since when are you friends with heads of drug cartels?"

Teresa laughed. She actually laughed, something she hadn't done in a long time. "Do you know where my bank book is?" She walked out of Vickie's room and into her own.

Vickie followed Teresa, in shock. "What is going on?"

"Nothing really, I'm tired of sitting around."

"So, you called a drug lord?"

Again, Teresa laughed. "I suppose I did. But he was in town so he came by."

"And how did he know where you were?"

She looked at her, raising her eyebrows. "I didn't ask him. But I'm sure the fact that you and your computer friend were looking for his number tipped him off. How did you get that number anyway?"

Vickie sat down on her bed. "I found it in your jewelry box. I wasn't trying to pry, just wanted to make sure you were okay. Teresa, what the hell is going on?"

Teresa sat down next to her. "He is looking for someone for me. Someone I can't forget."

"The someone who sent the postcard?"

Teresa nodded. "Yes. I thought he forgot me. I thought he left me and didn't want me. But when I saw the card, I knew it was from him."

"Who is him?"

Teresa smiled again. "He is who he is. I can't tell you now, but someday, I will tell you everything. Now, do you know where my bank book is?"

"I think Mom still has it."

"Great, will you take me over there so I can get it?"

Vickie nodded and got up. They walked into their parents' home, which shocked their mother. "Well, hello, girls, what brings you by? Vickie, why aren't you at work?"

"I took the day off today to hang out with Teresa."

"Hi, Mom," Teresa said and went to hug her. "Listen, I need my bank book and any identification you have of mine. My passport, anything."

"We have everything, sweetie. May I ask what you need it for?"

She smiled. "You can ask, but right now, I just want to go back into the world, and I need money and identification to do it."

Her mother gave her a funny look and went to her bedroom. When she came back, she had Teresa's purse. "Oh, my purse! Where did you get this?"

"The police gave it to me. They said they found it in the bathroom of the courthouse."

Teresa dumped everything on the table and then proceeded to rip the purse apart. She dropped what looked like a tracker on the table, then she found a microphone sewn into the lining. She picked them up and went to the sink, turning on the water and dropping them in. When she turned on the garbage disposal, her mother and sister just stood there watching in horror. Teresa came back and took her bank book, her driver's license, and her passport, then threw everything else away.

She kissed her mother on the cheek and hugged her. "Thanks, Mom. I will call you soon." Then she walked out the door. Sitting in Vickie's car waiting for her, she went over the last twenty-four hours.

Walking with purpose to the corner, she found a pay phone. With her hands shaking, she dialed the number that was seared into her mind.

"Yes," the voice said.

"Hello." She spoke softly.

"Ah, Teresa. It's so nice to hear your lovely voice. Is everything all right? How are you doing?" he asked.

"I'm afraid I am not doing so well, hence this phone call. I was wondering if we could have a private conversation."

"Of course, I would enjoy seeing your beautiful face again. I am in town on business, but I will make the time to see you. Tomorrow." He hung up.

She stood there looking at the receiver in her hand. What had she done? Why had she called him? But she knew why. She was desperate. She wanted him, needed him. He made her feel whole. He made her feel.

Teresa hung up the phone and went for a long walk, trying to calm her jittery nerves. Then she found a little store and bought some ice cream before going back home.

After talking with her sister, she went to bed. But sleep was not something that came easy that night. The fear she felt months ago, when she'd first met him in that abandoned building, was very real. He was a powerful man who could take her if he wanted, and no one would ever know where she was. But he was also a man of honor. Stone seemed to trust and respect him, and she had no other choice if she wanted to find him. He would know how; he would help her. The question was, what was she willing to pay for his help? Anything. If she was being honest with herself, she knew she would pay anything to find him again.

When she woke up, she took a shower and had some coffee. As she stood at the window looking out at Vickie's neighborhood, a gentle quiet knock came. Turning around, she knew who it was. This was it. Her heart raced as she moved without effort to the door. She opened it, and there he was, bigger than life, bigger than she remembered.

"Ah, beautiful Teresa," he said as he reached up to run his finger along her jaw.

She didn't want him to touch her, but she knew he would respect her. "Please, come in," she said in a tiny voice.

His smile lit up the room, and he walked past her. She half-expected a few of his henchmen to walk in behind him, but no one was there, so she shut the door and followed him into the living room. She stood in front of the window, trying to form the words.

"What has marred this lovely face in such a way?" he asked as he moved closer to her.

"I need your help, but I am afraid to ask for it. I don't have anything to pay you with."

He chuckled. "Being in your presence is more than enough payment. I am not a monster. I would never take something that isn't offered freely, and I would most definitely never take what belonged to someone else."

She half-smiled. "Well, that's just it. I don't know if I belong to anyone."

He laughed. "Oh, Hermosa, no matter what the show was that my friend Stone put on, I could see the love in his eyes. I could see it in yours in that dreadful hallway all those months ago. You belong to him, and he is a very lucky man."

She smiled. "I need a starting point. I am healed now, and I need to know so I can move on with my life, whether it with him or not. I have no idea where to begin. This is a big world, and I am afraid I do not have the resources it will take to find him. I just need some place to begin."

He smiled at her in a loving manner, cupping her face in his hand. "Ah, love, I remember it with my wife. She was all I could think about. To this day, making love to her still brings tears to my eyes."

This confused her. Why would he want a submissive if he loved his wife? He chuckled at the face she made.

"My wife is a gentle soul. Me, well, I like a bit of... shall we say, excitement. She is understanding." Teresa nodded. "I will help you."

Just then, the door flew open and Vickie came in, as he ran his finger along her cheek. "I will do whatever I can to help you. You will owe me nothing. I am jealous of my old friend. You are a rare beauty. I will do my best. Have a good life, Hermosa." he said to her. Leaning in, he kissed her forehead. Then turned to face Vickie. Smiling at her, he said, "Ah, the sister. Perhaps you should keep your things well-hidden, Hermosa. Your sister tried to find me today." He walked by, touching her frozen face. "Lovely, just like your sister," he said to her.

"I'm sorry, it won't happen again," Teresa said softly.

Carlos turned to her, smiling. "Nonsense, I told you, just as I told our mutual friend, whatever you need. You did me a great service, and I will forever be grateful. I hope to see you one day again. Remember, a fine line. I could bring you the greatest pleasure you have ever known."

Teresa smiled at him. "No, thank you. As I said before, I think I've had my fair share of pain."

Carlos nodded and walked out the door.

~

Vickie opened the car door, jolting her out of her daydream. "Sweetie, you are scaring the shit out of me with all this secrecy. What in the hell is going on?"

"Vic, I hope you didn't mention our visitor to Mom."

"Are you kidding me? I'm not that stupid."

Teresa smiled and they drove home in silence.

The next morning Vickie went to work and Teresa went to the bank. She withdrew twenty thousand of her forty-eight and then went to the local department store. She bought a bag, a few pairs of jeans, some shirts, a bathing suit, some bras, and panties. She finished off her new wardrobe with a pair of tennis shoes, a pair of boots, a baseball cap, some new sunglasses, and some hoodies. When she checked out, she asked the girl at the register if she could remove all the tags for her and then put everything in the bag. After she paid, she went to the bathroom and changed her clothes, dumping her old things in the garbage before heading home.

Days passed, turning into a week. One morning, she got up and found a piece of paper lying on the floor by the front door. Her hand shook as she bent and picked it up. Written on the paper were three words.

Remember the path.

She stood there looking at it, trying to figure out what it meant. Then it hit her. She wrote Vickie a note.

I love you all. Please, don't look for me. I am fine. I will be in touch. Promise.

T.

She grabbed her bag, put her money and identification in it, grabbed the postcard and the card from her jewelry box, and left her sister's house. Grabbing a cab, she went to the old, abandoned building down the street from The Black Cat. She shivered as she remembered that night and what she had done. She followed the path to the rundown hotel. Going in, she got a room and then went out the side door. She moved down the street until she found another cab, then went to the train station. She went in and bought a ticket to Oklahoma. After making her way down to the platform, she found the exit door and took it, making sure she wasn't seen. Maneuvering her way through the tunnels and the pedways, she exited at the Thompson Center on LaSalle Street. A cab was waiting on the street, so she took it to Grant Park. Slowly, she made her way down and across Lake Shore Drive to the marina.

She didn't have a pass key to get in so she waited. A family came by, and she followed them in. Doing her best not to be seen, she followed the path to the end of the marina. The boat in the last slip of the dock was not the same one they were in before. She just stood there waiting to make sure she was doing the right thing.

A man appeared, obviously not an American, and nodded to her. She climbed aboard and moved into the cabin. The boat took off a few minutes later. She found a life jacket and put it on. They drove out into the lake for about an hour then slowed down, and the engines eventually shut off. The man came to find her. "Come," he said.

She followed him onto the deck and found that they were next to a huge yacht. After climbing up, she was ushered into a helicopter that was on the top of the yacht. Once in the chopper, it fired up and took off. They flew to what looked like an abandoned airfield in the middle of nowhere.

She was then put on a private jet. When she walked on the plane, there were six other women on it. Some were dressed up and some looked like they were scared shitless. She imagined her face looked the same. Another man walked her to the back of the plane, to a bedroom. "You stay here," he said to her, shutting the door on the way out.

Teresa was now in full blown panic mode. She knew she would have to pay for this; she just didn't want it to be this way. Sitting in the chair, she took off her life jacket and buckled her seat belt. The plane took off. A lovely woman came in and offered her something to eat and drink. She opted not to have anything, for fear it would be drugged.

Hours and hours went by, and no one came to her. She felt the plane slow and start to land. There was a window, but she didn't want to look out. When the plane landed, she waited. The same man came for her. "You come now," he said, so she got up, grabbed her bag, and followed him out.

As she was walking down the stairs, she noticed the other girls getting into black SUVs. The man opened a door in the last one, signaling for her to get in. She did. The windows were blacked out so she couldn't see anything. They drove for about an hour. When the car stopped, her door opened, and Carlos was standing there ready to greet her.

"Ah, the beautiful Teresa. Welcome to my home. I trust you had a good journey." He took her hand and kissed the back of it.

She was terrified. What had she done? There was no way she would ever get out of here alive. She was in Columbia.

"Come, you can freshen up, have a meal, meet my wife, and your journey will continue in the morning." He smiled at her, leading her up to the house.

She noticed the other SUVs continue on to the back of the house. Well, it wasn't a house; it was a fortress, walled with armed guards, men walking around with what looked like machine guns. He walked her right in the front door where his wife was waiting. She was breathtakingly beautiful. He introduced them, and then a maid took her upstairs to a bedroom. She showered and changed her clothes, neatly putting the others in her bag. Feeling out of place, she sat down in a chair and waited.

She was terrified as to what could happen to her here. But she let her mind wander to him. To the possibility of seeing him, touching him, making love to him. She felt her face flush at the thought of his mouth on her. The door opened, but she didn't notice until a voice snapped her out of her thoughts.

"What I wouldn't give to see that beautiful rose color, knowing I was the one who put it there," Carlos said in a very seductive voice. Teresa turned to face him, smiling. "I've come to walk you down to dinner." He reached his hand out to her. She took it and let him escort her to the dining room. Sitting at the table were his wife and four daughters, who were equally as beautiful as their mother.

They said a prayer in Spanish and then ate. Carlos watched her pick at her food and smiled at her. "This is what you have done for me," he said, waving his hand around the table. "My daughters are a bit safer in this world now. A man such as Sully needed to be ended. He was a greedy man."

Teresa nodded. "Thank you for helping me, and for your hospitality, but I am rather tired and would like to go to bed." He nodded. "What time will we be leaving in the morning?"

"When you are ready to go, you can go," he replied.

She chuckled, "I am ready now."

"If that is the case, then we shall make it happen." He stood, walking over to her chair and pulling it out for her. "I will get everything ready for you. It was an honor having you grace my home with your beauty," he said as he walked her to the stairs.

Teresa smiled and nodded to him. She went upstairs and got her bag, and then met him again at the bottom of the stairs. "Come, your ride awaits you. My men will see you all the way to your destination. From there, you will find your own way." He put a card in her hand. "Find this place and you will find what you search for. Remember, I am always here if you find that it is not what you want. I can give you a fine life."

"Thank you, for everything." She leaned in and kissed him on the cheek. He touched her face and then opened the door, and Teresa walked out and down the stairs.

Climbing into the car, she took one last look at the powerful man who had helped her. She just wanted to get the hell out of here. The journey was long across South America. For days and days, they drove, stopping only to refuel, use the restroom, and to get food. She had no idea where she was going. On the afternoon of the seventh day, they pulled up to a hotel.

The driver got out and opened her door. "This is a safe place for you to sleep. We will be in town until you find what your heart desires, per our orders. We will watch out for you until you find what it is you are looking for. You will not see us, but we will see you. Good luck, Miss," he said as she climbed out of the car.

"Thank you," she whispered and walked into the hotel to get a room. Once inside, she took a shower and changed her clothes. She was so very tired, but she wanted to go find out if what she was feeling was the truth. She walked out onto the street and started toward her destination. It was just a few blocks away. She could hear the bells from the boats along the shore as she walked. It was late in the day, and she was hungry. Once she found the place she was looking for, with shaking hands, she pulled open the door and walked in. The outside of the building led her to believe it was a crappy little bar, but when she walked inside, she was pleasantly surprised to find it was a very nice place. There was a bar on one side and a restaurant of sorts on the other. She knew enough Spanish to get herself through. A lovely young woman seated her at a table across the room from the door. She ordered some food and sat in the near darkness with her cap on, her hair hidden from view, with her hoodie concealing her tiny frame. This had become her look since she left home.

She stayed at the restaurant until nightfall and then went back to her hotel. Day after day, she went for breakfast, lunch, and dinner. Along the way, she shopped at some little shops and just kept to herself. The days dragged on, her hopes becoming less and less as each day passed. Eighteen days she had been in this little community. The people at the restaurant were becoming familiar to her routine. And that is just what it was. A routine. She needed to stop wishing he would come. She knew this was a long shot. Did Carlos do this on purpose? Was he hoping to dash all of her thoughts and then bring her back to him?

On her walk back to the hotel, she found herself at the water's edge. The boats that lined the shore were small and very sad looking. Children played in the water wearing very little. Couples walked along the beach holding hands. She found a place to sit and just watched. Time flew by, and she found herself a bit hungry so she headed back to the restaurant. She was seated in her usual place and was just finishing her meal. As she got up to leave, she heard a huge laugh coming from the bar.

She froze in her tracks. She couldn't see into the bar from where she stood. Inching closer, she heard a female voice.

"Well, my American friend, it has been a long time. Someone has been looking for you. Miss Charlotte is sitting in the back."

"Well, Maria, it is good to see you as well. I have been busy lately, so my trips to the mainland have been few."

"Yes, but what about Miss Charlotte?" she said.

Then Teresa heard another woman's voice. "There you are. Where have you been? I have missed you."

Teresa walked into view of the bar and watched the scene in front of her. It was him. It was really him. Her heart stopped. She nearly ran to him, but a beautiful blonde woman walked up and draped herself over him, kissing him on the mouth. He pulled back and smiled at her. "Now, Charlotte, we have been over this before."

She pouted at him, inches from his face. "Yes, but you are a lonely man and I am in need. How can you resist me?"

He wrapped his arm around her waist, pulling her to him, and whispered in her ear, "The heart wants what the heart wants."

The woman connected eyes with Teresa as she laughed, swatting him on the arm. Then she snuggled into his embrace. Teresa stood there frozen. She wasn't sure if she was pissed, shocked, or hurt. Without realizing it, her feet were moving toward him. She was but five feet from him, and he froze, letting go of the woman in his arms.

The hair on his neck stood up, an electricity of sorts energizing in his body. He slowly turned on his stool to look behind him, but there was no one there.

Teresa had thought twice about approaching him because he looked so happy. She turned and bolted out of the restaurant. Running into the street, she felt her stomach turn and her dinner came up.

Charlotte said to him, "What's the matter, darling?"

"Did you see anyone standing there?" He pointed to the door.

"A little waif of a girl in some kind of sweatshirt with a hood on. Why?"

He pushed her away and got off his stool, running out into the street. There was no one there. He stepped off the sidewalk into the street. He saw the vomit on the street and panicked. "No, no," he whispered to himself. *Could it be?* He wondered. Searching the street, he saw nothing.

He shook his head and went back into the bar. Teresa was standing on the side of the building, wiping the tears from her eyes. She didn't know what to do. She had come here to find him, to see if he wanted her, but he was wrapped up in the blonde. She came here to find out. She needed to get on with her life; it had been months of nothing inside of her but him. She needed to do this. If he didn't want her, at least she would know. She would go back to Chicago and move on with her life.

Taking a few deep breaths, she made herself move.

When he went back in, Charlotte looked at him. "You look like you saw a ghost."

He looked at her. "You could say that."

"Who hurt you so badly that you and I can't enjoy ourselves?" She snuggled up to him again.

"She didn't hurt me. I am the one who hurt her. I left her, gave her back her life. A life I didn't fit into," he said with a sad voice.

"For months we have known one another, and for months you have been alone. You have needs, and I can fulfill them for you," she whispered in his ear.

He chuckled. "I'm afraid she ruined me for any woman other than her. It is never going to happen, Charlotte. I'm sorry. You are very beautiful and desirable, but you are not her."

Teresa walked back into the bar. She didn't pause and she didn't hesitate, just walked right up to him and placed her hand on his back. His body stiffened. Charlotte said, "What's the matter, did you change your mind?"

He pushed her away. He knew this feeling of electricity engulfing his body. He slowly turned, and Teresa dropped her hoodie and took off her cap. He swore he was dreaming; the air caught in his lungs. She was here. She was right in front of him. He looked into her eyes and saw she had been crying. There were tears in them now.

"Oh God," he whispered. "No, beautiful, it is not what you think." His hands moved on their own to cup her face, pulling her to him. He covered her mouth with his. He was home. He would never let her go. She came to find him. She really wanted him. He felt it in her kiss. Pulling away, he watched as more tears fell from her eyes, and he wiped them away with his thumbs. He pulled her into his embrace. Her hands wrapping around his waist, she laid her head on his chest, hearing his heart slam against it. He pulled her back, looking at her and kissed her again.

"Excuse me," they heard. But he didn't stop kissing her. Elation was not a word he ever dreamed he would feel. Someone tapped him on the shoulder. "Hey, what about me? I was here first."

Teresa smiled and pulled back, whispering in his mouth, "I think someone wants you."

"I am hoping it's you," he whispered back, smiling.

She nodded. "Yes, always."

He turned with Teresa in his arms. "I'm sorry, ladies, but I need to go." He looked at the bartender. "Maria, it was good to see you." He laid some money on the bar. "Charlotte, thanks but no thanks." He stood up and wrapped his arm around Teresa's waist, and they walked out the door.

"I have a room up the street. We can talk there, if you want. Otherwise, I can meet you in the morning someplace," she offered.

He laughed. "Come on, I will walk you home." They didn't say anything while they walked the few blocks. He didn't let her go until they went in her room. He looked around, picked up her bag, and put what little things she had brought with her in it. He walked over and kissed her. "Come home with me," he said.

She nodded, and he kissed her again. Together, hand in hand, they walked back to the docks. He helped her in his boat, and they headed out to sea. She didn't say anything, just sat in the boat with her life-jacket on, watching him. The sun was nearly gone, making it pitch black on the sea. She was scared, but he was with her. In the distance, she could see a small light, and as they moved across the water, it got bigger and brighter. Soon, they were slowing down and pulling up to a small dock. He helped her out and then covered the boat. Together, they walked down the dock. He hit a switch at the end and turned off the light, blanketing them in total darkness.

Her grip tightened around his hand, and he smiled. They walked along the beach for a few minutes, and then he turned them into what looked like a jungle. A few feet in, she saw little lights along the path. He led her along the path for about ten minutes before coming out into a small clearing when the lights on the path disappeared. He stopped, pulling her to him, dropping her bag on the ground and kissing her. "Welcome to my home," he whispered against her lips.

Letting her go, he picked up her bag and continued walking. They walked up a few steps and then onto a porch. He opened the door and turned on the lights. Teresa stood there, completely amazed at what she was seeing. White marble floors, white walls where there were walls, but mostly it was open to the outside. A breeze blew white sheers inward. As they moved through the place, she saw a huge white leather sectional and a full gourmet kitchen. He led her down a hall to a set of double doors and pushed them open, revealing his bedroom. In the center of the room was the biggest bed she had ever seen. It had mosquito netting all the way around it, so much and so long it piled in bunches on the floor. He moved ahead of her, putting her bag on a bench at the foot of the bed.

"The bathroom is in here. I will sleep in the spare room if you want, but I want you to sleep here." He walked up to her. "I want you to sleep in my bed." After kissing her once more, he walked to the doors. "I will leave you to it. I'll be back in a little bit with something to eat. Make yourself at home." He pulled the doors closed, leaving her alone in his room.

Teresa stood there, awestruck. It had been months since she had seen him. He acted like they had never been apart. There was so much to talk about, so much to be said. But she was tired and dirty. She made her way to the bathroom, where she showered and then wrapped herself in a towel and went to climb into bed. She was so exhausted from being afraid. For the first time in a year, she felt comfortable. She felt at peace. She felt safe. Sleep found her easily and soundly.

Tate came back into the room with some food and found her sleeping, wrapped in a towel. His heart fluttered. She looked so beautiful and so tiny in his bed. He set the tray down and went to shower. When he came out, he sat in the chair and watched her sleep in the soft glow of the little light by his bed. For hours, he watched her. He wanted to climb in next to her and hold her, but he wouldn't do that unless she wanted it. He still didn't know how she found him. How long had she been there? There was so much they needed to talk about. How long was she going to stay? Was she here for work? Months ago, he had sent that card, and nothing. Now, here she was, in his bed, on his island.

She moved and rolled over, facing him. Her towel came undone. The curve of her hip triggered something inside of him. He could feel the heat start to burn. His cock grew harder as his eyes moved up her body. Her breast, with its puckered nipple, called to him. As his eyes moved up to her face, they locked with hers. He got up slowly, moving the netting as he climbed onto the bed. Her hand came up to touch his face.

"You are so fucking beautiful," he whispered as he positioned himself next to her.

"Tate," she said softly. "It's really you?"

"Yeah, beautiful, it's me." He laid on his side, pulling her to him. His leg went between hers, and she put hers on his hip. Wrapping his arms around her, pressing her chest against his, he covered her mouth with his. The kiss was gentle and tender. He loved the taste of her on his mouth. He was home, a home he never knew, a home he dreamed of for months.

They lay there kissing for some time. His cock was as hard as stone against her tiny stomach. He could feel her on his thigh, her hips rubbing gently on him every now and then. There was nothing rushed, nothing hurried. Just the two of them holding each other and kissing. He moved his hand down her side to her hip and back again, time and time again. He couldn't believe she was here, but he still didn't know why, after all this time. Right now, it was something he needed to know. He couldn't make love to her if she was here to bring him back. He didn't want to believe that, but it was a possibility.

He pulled out of the kiss, bringing his hand up to run his thumb across her lips. They were a bit swollen from his kisses. "Beautiful," he whispered to her. She closed her eyes as the tears came. He felt very uncomfortable suddenly. Fear welled up inside of him. Was she going to break his heart?

She opened her eyes and looked deep into his. He saw the fear in hers. She untangled herself from him, pulling her towel around herself, and sat up facing him.

"Why did you leave me?" she whispered.

He sat up, his cock standing straight up. But he didn't care. He didn't even try to cover it up. "I made a promise to you."

"I don't understand."

"I told you I would get you home to your family. I did that. I couldn't just let you walk away. You needed to be found with the other women. I didn't want you to be implicated in what we did in that building. You needed to have your life back, and ending the lives of eleven men would have put you in prison. Then we would have had to break you out, and you would never have gotten your life back." He spoke very quietly, very carefully, very gently, touching her with every word he said.

"Beautiful, we had to get Kelly and get out of the country before anyone knew we were there. I must admit, we wouldn't have been able to explain anything to them. What was happening went a lot deeper than just Sully and Ted. There were a lot of people involved. Stone left the file for the F.B.I. Didn't you see the news?"

She shook her head. "I couldn't."

"Oh, beautiful," he said, leaning in to kiss her.

"Why didn't you come for me?"

"Because you needed to heal. You had been through so much, done so much. I needed for you to become you again. Not the broken, scared, defiled woman I knew. But the strong, independent force of nature you were."

"I will never be that woman again."

"I'm so sorry for that."

She nodded, wiping the tears from her eyes. "Do you want me still?" she whispered, looking down at her lap.

He lifted her face. "What do you think?"

"I don't know what to think. I know that we are definitely compatible in bed. But do you want me, the woman before you? The broken, insecure, frightened woman who sits before you?"

He smiled. "With every fiber of my being. I have wanted you since that night I picked you up off the road. You have been in here," he touched his heart, "all these months, even when I thought you didn't want me. I thought I did the right thing by putting you in that truck. I never expected to see you again. I sent that card a few weeks after I left you. I thought you didn't want me."

"Who was that woman in the bar?"

"An American who lives down here. She has been after me since the first day I walked into the place."

"Is she your lover?"

He shook his head. "My heart belongs to you."

Teresa froze. "Uh," she breathed out.

He sat there looking at her. Swallowing hard, he whispered, "I love you, beautiful. I knew it that very first time. I knew it when I put you in that truck. I was broken for so long, but you healed me."

She threw herself into his arms, searing his lips with a kiss. Wrapping his arms around her, he held on. Teresa managed to straddle him, rubbing her center on his cock. A growl came from deep inside him.

She pushed up on her knees until she reached the tip of his head, then she slid down, taking him all the way to his balls.

He moaned as her silk surrounded him. "Oh God, beautiful." She made love to him. He laid her down on the bed, pulling out of her. She felt the loss of him and moaned. He moved down her body with his mouth. "I want to taste you, every inch of you," he whispered over her nipple and then engulfed it in his mouth.

"Ahh," she cried out. "Oh God, Tate, I'm going to come."

He smiled and moved to the other one. Drawing it in his mouth so slowly, he savored the feel of her taut nipple on his tongue. He felt her hips come off the bed as she combusted. Her hands were in his hair, tugging the strands. He was going to explode right into the mattress. He moved down to her stomach, kissing her scars, lingering on her belly button.

Then he positioned himself between her legs, spreading her wide. He dipped his face in her fluff of hair and inhaled. "You smell like heaven," he said as his fingers opened her lips to expose her swollen little pink bud for him. He flicked it with his tongue.

"Ahh," she cried out.

He gently moved his mouth closer, wrapping his lips around it and moaning when he fully tasted her. He held her nub in his lips and flicked it with his tongue. Her legs tightened, and he knew she was going to come again. He flattened his tongue and started little circles on her most sensitive spot. His fingers found her wet, and as soon as he pushed in, he hooked them so he could rub her g-spot. It only took seconds before she came unraveled, moaning and shaking as her orgasm ripped through her. Tate moved his mouth to her opening and covered it, sucking all she had to give him. His tongue pushed deep inside of her, making sure he got every last drop of her golden honey.

She pushed her hands in his hair, pulling him up her body. When his mouth met hers, she devoured him. He pushed so slowly inside of her, releasing instantly, filling her with his own orgasm. Completely drained and sedate, they fell asleep almost instantly wrapped in each other.

When he moved, she moved with him. They slept the entire day.

Teresa woke first. She needed to use the bathroom and she was hungry. She managed to get out of bed and to the bathroom. Once she turned on the shower, Tate was standing behind her. He wrapped his arms around her, palming her nipples. Together, they showered and enjoyed each other.

He took her from behind with her hands on the shower wall. Thrusting up into her, he lifted her off the floor. "Fuck me," she cried out as he thrust into her. Tate wrapped his arm around her waist and slammed into her. She screamed out, "Yes," again and again he fucked her, until he couldn't hold back any more. He reached down and touched her clit, sending her over the edge with him. Their bodies jerked as they came together.

Teresa leaned against his chest, bringing her arms up around his neck. "You own me," she whispered to him.

He pulled out and turned her around. Kissing her, he told her, "No, beautiful, you own me."

They washed again and got out. Tate dressed in a pair of shorts. "I'll be in the kitchen," he said to her as he walked out of the bedroom. She smiled at him and nodded. Teresa towel-dried her hair and then put on a pair of shorts and a t-shirt. She didn't bother with the bra and panties; she didn't plan on going anywhere.

Slowly, she walked out into the living area of this huge but comfortable house. She stood leaning against the wall, watching him in the kitchen. His body was bare, his legs and feet bare. As he moved around the stove, his back and shoulder muscles flexed. He reached for something, and the muscles in his legs got rock hard. He was fucking beautiful. No wonder that woman in the bar wanted him. Hell, if she were dead, she would want him. She walked up behind him and kissed his back, wrapping her arms around his stomach. He put his hand on hers.

"I poured you some juice."

She kissed his back again. "Thank you."

She walked around the massive island and picked up the glass of juice, and continued through the living room to the open wall and out onto the deck. The view was spectacular. The palm trees swayed in the gentle breeze, giving her a clear view of the ocean. You couldn't see the mainland from here, so she suspected it was on the other side of the house.

Tate turned to put the food on the island and looked up. Her tiny body standing in the sunlight caused him to lose his breath. Her tiny shorts hugged her beautiful ass. The gap between her legs made him instantly hard. She turned to look at him. She had on a thin, white, tiny t-shirt, her nipples showing through it, taut and wanton of his mouth. He smiled at her.

"Come on and eat beautiful," he said. Watching her walk toward him, her hips swayed just a little, her breasts swaying perfectly. He moaned inwardly.

They sat and ate, looking at each other and smiling every now and again. When they finished, she started clearing the island and then doing the dishes.

"I can do that," he offered.

"Don't be silly, you just cooked all this food. I can do it."

He laughed and got up to go out on the deck. He needed to gather the right words to find out why she was there. He was on high alert, a tenseness he hadn't felt since he got here. How did she find him? He sat in a chaise lounge, warring with himself on how to find out.

When she finished, she came out and climbed on top of him, snuggling into his chest. He wrapped his arms around her and held her close. She was the one who spoke first.

"Tate?"

"Yeah, beautiful."

"Do you want me here?"

"Why would you ask me that?"

"I don't know, it's just a feeling I am getting from you. It's like you're not sure if you want me here. I feel like I'm intruding. I mean, if there is someone else, I would understand. I came here to see if you felt the same way I did."

He felt her trembling. She was terrified of what he was going to say.

"Hey," he said, lifting her face to his. "I want you here. I am just wondering, I guess."

"About what?"

"About how long you are going to stay. Please, don't take this the wrong way, but why now? Why did you wait so long to come?"

She pushed up, getting up and walking to the railing. She didn't know what to say to him. Teresa thought the fact that she was here was obvious to him. Maybe he thought something else. She was struggling with how to say what she should say without him feeling sorry for her. She had been a pathetic excuse for a woman, pining away for him for months. Sad, disappointed and pissed off that he would take what she gave him and then just leave her. Looking around, she saw some stairs that led off the porch, so she turned and walked to them and down onto the grass. She kept walking, not knowing where she was going but needing to gather her thoughts, needing to figure out a way not to sound so pathetic. If he felt sorry for her, it wouldn't be the same as if he understood.

He did tell her last night that he loved her. Was he just saying that? God, all this speculation. She was an educated woman with a brain. But she was terrified of how she felt, how she would come off. If he didn't want her, it would devastate her. She knew men who would easily take sex from her. Is that what this was? They were good in bed. God were they good. She had felt nothing like it in her life, but is that all it was? She had walked all the way to the beach and sat down in the sand. How would she tell him that she had no life back home, that she didn't ever want to leave him? Would he want that? Would he want the broken woman she was now?

She felt him walk up. It amazed her that she could feel him before he even touched her. Was that love, or was it just the energy the two of them had together?

He sat beside her, not touching her and not saying a word. She decided she would just start talking.

"When we left that building and we were in the alley and you kissed me, there was so much I wanted to say to you, but you started to undress me. It hit me what you were doing, that you were going to leave me. My heart stopped. My mind stopped. I couldn't figure out why you would do that. Then you kissed me goodbye and put me in that truck, shutting the door. I couldn't look at you. I couldn't breathe. Days and days went by while I was in that hospital, days I don't remember. My family wanted nothing more than to help me, and I couldn't stand for them to be near me, always wanting to touch me, to hug me.

"I felt dirty and alone. All I could do was cry. I wanted you to come and get me. I hoped you wanted me. I waited, thinking you were waiting for some time to pass, waiting until it was safe. But weeks and weeks went by. I sat in a chair in front of the window in my sister's apartment, just waiting. I would cry myself to sleep every night waiting for you to come. I couldn't accept the fact that you didn't want me. After everything we had been through, after making love all those times, especially the last time on that boat, I was sure you would come.

"I couldn't talk to anyone about what happened, about what we shared, about how I felt about you. I was in hell and alone. Weeks turned into months and nothing. No sign of you. I couldn't go out of the house because the press wouldn't let me breathe. I couldn't go back to work. It's not who I am anymore. What happened ruined me, took every bit of confidence I had away from me. I felt like a hollow human being. I had nothing except the memories.

"Then a little over a month ago, my sister came home with a huge box of cards that my mother had given her. They were from people all over the place wishing me well. Day after day, she would read them to me while I sat in the chair staring out the window, wondering where you were, what you were doing. Wondering if you were missing me. Hell, I was wondering if you were even thinking about me. I mean, look at you. You could have any woman you wanted, so why would you want me? I am so broken now, seriously broken. Everything I was is gone."

Tate wanted to grab her and kiss her, but he didn't. She needed to say this to him, and he needed to know.

"Well, one night, she said, 'Oh, a postcard.' She had mentioned it didn't have a stamp on it. Then she read it. 'Thinking of you.' To be honest, my heart started beating again at that moment. I felt my body get warmer. I had been so cold since that night, feeling nothing but emptiness. I missed you so badly, Tate. I was so sure we were just what it was, two people stuck in a situation, and sex was our release. I actually convinced myself at one point that I had suffered from a form of Stockholm syndrome.

"But she sat the card down on the table next to me. I didn't want to look at it, because I was terrified to feel excited. But my eyes were drawn to it. It was like a beacon. When I saw the palm tree with the sunlight shining through the leaves, my breath caught. It took me a few minutes to pull myself together, and then I got up and left.

"I did something I might one day regret, but I didn't care. I needed to know. I needed to see you. I need to know now, Tate. I need to know if you want me, if you want this woman I have become. I am terrified of the way that I feel for you. If you send me away, I will crumble, but at least I will know and can pick up the pieces and try to move on with my life."

Tate wiped the tears from his cheeks, pulling her on top of his lap. "Yes," he said as he kissed her. "Yes, I want you. Yes, I need you. Yes, I want you always. There has been no one else, and there will never be anyone else. It's been you since that day in the road. It's been you since that first kiss. No woman will ever own me the way you do."

He kissed her again through her tears, but she pulled back. "I love you so much. I don't even know how it happened, but I don't think I can survive without you in my life."

He laid her back on the sand and kissed her long and deep. They laid there kissing for a long time, taking their time with one another, something they never really had. All of their moments were brief but powerful enough to bond them together.

Tate rolled over on his back, pulling her on top of him, and they laid in the sand, him moving his hands up and down her body. He couldn't believe she was here, and she wanted to stay. "So, what you are saying to me is you want to stay here with me?"

"Yes," she answered.

"On this island?"

"Yes."

"Just you and me?"

"Yes."

"And you love me?"

"Yes."

"You want this boring life with me?"

"Yes."

He wrapped his arms around her, hugging her tightly. "You have no plans to leave me?"

"Not unless you want me to go."

"That, beautiful, is never going to happen. I want you."

"Broken?"

He chuckled. "Yes, even broken."

She picked her head up and smiled at him. "Make love to me, Tate."

He kissed her, gently rolling her over. Slowly, he peeled off her shirt and shorts, then took his off. He took her slowly on the sand, until they were breathless and sedate. They lay there wrapped in each other for hours, naked on the sand.

He chuckled. "You are going to get burnt if you aren't already. Come on, let's go take a shower and grab something to eat."

He helped her up, grabbing their clothes, and they walked naked back to the house. They showered in the outside shower and made love again. She put on one of his t-shirts, and they made lunch together.

He looked at her as she put the dishes in the sink. "You said on the beach that you did something you might regret. You never did tell me how you found me."

She stopped mid-rinse, turned off the water, dried her hands, and walked out onto the deck. Tate watched her, wondering what she had done. He followed her out, standing right behind her.

"I think I might have sold my soul to Satan himself."

Tate's breath froze in his lungs as he waited for her to finish.

"That night, when we were in the hall, he put something in my hand. Something I held onto. It was the only tangible thing I had to remind me it was all real. To remind me that you were real, that this between us, was real. When I saw the postcard, I was desperate. I needed to know, Tate. I needed to know you were real. I needed to know if what I felt was real, or if I was just suffering from all the trauma."

He didn't say anything. He closed his eyes, trying not to react to his stupid decision to walk away from her. He was the cause of this part of her suffering. He was the reason she couldn't go on.

"Carlos," she said quietly.

Tate swallowed. "What do you mean?"

"In the hallway, when he said goodbye to us, he put a card in my hand. It had a number on it. The day I saw the postcard, I went for a walk and called him. He came the next day and told me he would help me. When I went to my parents' and got my identification, I found a tracker and a bug imbedded in my purse, so I put them in the garbage disposal and threw everything else out. The next day, I went to the bank and withdrew twenty thousand dollars, so I was ready to go when he contacted me. Then I went to the store and bought a new bag, new shoes, and new clothes. I changed in the store and threw everything I was wearing in the garbage. I went home and waited. Finally, one morning, I got up, and there was a note on the floor that simply said, 'follow the path.' It took me a few minutes to figure out what it meant."

"The path we took that night to the marina?"

"Yes, so I did everything you did. When I got to the marina, I got on a boat that took me out into the lake to another boat. I got on a helicopter that took me to an airfield. There, I boarded a private jet filled with women. I was escorted to the back of the plane to a private bedroom. When we landed, I got in a car and was driven to his home. I met his wife and daughters and then started my journey here. His men stayed in town to watch over me until I found you. I have been here for nearly three weeks looking for you. All I had was the address to the bar. Then, well, now I am here."

He turned her around and smothered her with his mouth. "You brave, crazy, beautiful girl. I don't even know what to say."

"Say you are all right with my decision to find you. Say it's all right I trusted him. Say you want me to stay here with you. I can't go back, Tate. I can't live in this life without you."

"Yes." He kissed her. "Yes." He kissed her again. "Yes." He kissed her again. Lifting her up to sit on the railing, he dropped his shorts and took her, slamming deep into her, kissing her. With every breath he took, he said yes to her, while he fucked her hard and slow.

When they finished, he carried her into the house and they snuggled on the couch. She lay on top of him while he ran his fingers up and down her body. "I need to get word to my sister, to let her know I am alive."

"I can do that. Are you going to tell her where you are?"

"Yes, I am going to tell her I am with the man I love, living the life I want. But no, not where we are."

He smiled. "I'll make dinner while you write your letter." He kissed the top of her head. "There is paper in the desk in our room."

She froze. "Our room?"

"Yes, beautiful, our room. I don't ever want a day without you. This is your home now if you want it."

"I want it," she whispered as she kissed him.

He smacked her on the ass, and they laughed. She got up and went to the bedroom, finding the paper, and wrote her sister a letter.

Dear Vickie,

I know you are worried about me, but I am finally free of the torment I was in. I am with him now. It was a long journey to find him, but we are together now. I am finally at peace with all that happened to me.

He saved me, and then he kept his promise to give me back my life. But I discovered over the time I spent with you that my life wasn't complete without him. I believed he didn't want me. I think that is what made me so sad. I needed to take this journey to find out if I was just hanging onto something I wasn't sure was real.

Turns out, he feels the same way. I am happy, finally happy. I have no life back there. I can't do what I did before. I am not that same woman.

Please, tell Mom and Dad that I love them. I love you, and I am forever grateful you are my sister. One day, I will be back, and I will bring him with me. One day, you will see that I am a different person. It was very difficult for me to stand in everyone's judgement or to fulfill their expectations of what my life should be.

I am not crazy, nor was I ever. My heart was broken, and I felt lost without him. Now, I feel whole and accepted, and most of all, I am loved by him.

I can't write again, but you will always be in my thoughts and in my heart. I love you so much, and one day, we shall see each other again.

All of my love
   T.

She folded the paper and put it in an envelope, then made her way out to the kitchen. She wrapped her arms around Tate and kissed his back.

"You all right?" he asked her.

"I am now."

www.ingramcontent.com/pod-product-compliance
Lightning Source LLC
Chambersburg PA
CBHW022101170626
46808CB00002B/548